Girl, Recycled!

Yolanda T. McCray

ISBN: 978-1-7364145-0-7

The Pearl Agency
Georgetown, SC

*Cover and Interior design done by Tami Boyce
(www.tamiboyce.com)*

TABLE OF CONTENTS

Girl, Recycled!

GRADUATION DAY (PRESENT-DAY)

"Okay, everyone. Let's gather around for pictures. Tabitha, you and Paige get on either end. Lyric, Peyton, Isabella, Chloe, Courtney, and Amanda fill in between them. All my girls are together...you are gorgeous, and I am so proud of each of you," said Mama Timmons as she smiled ear to ear. "Is everybody ready? On the count of three, say Recycled."

One, two, three. "Recycled!" the girls exclaimed.

"I will treasure this moment for the rest of my life. I can't believe that you all have graduated. Time has flown by. You made it, Princesses!"

"So, what do we do now, Mama Timmons?" Tabitha asked.

"What do you mean, baby girl?"

"We have spent the last three and a half years of our life with you," Paige added.

"Yes, we have been here since the summer of our 10th-grade year," Peyton chimed in. It just seems so strange to be leaving now."

"I don't want to leave you, Mama Timmons," Lyric said as a teardrop fell from her eyes.

"Oh no, sweethearts, I don't ever want you to feel that way," Mama Timmons says as she tries to console her girls. "You aren't leaving me. I will always be here for you. It's time for you to fly now. Your wings are new, and you are ready to fly."

"But...what if we mess up?" Isabella asked.

"Then, you will get back up again, responded Mama Timmons. "You know how to do that now...Just remember everything that I have taught you over the past years. The eight of you have grown so much. I am confident in my God that you will do just fine. Do you girls remember when you first came to me?"

"Yes, we were all messed up," Amanda said.

"But take a good look at you now! No traces of dirt, scars, or brokenness."

"Except for Paige; don't forget about her ankle," Tabitha says jokingly.

"But seriously, girls, God has genuinely recycled and made each of you into a new person... Beautiful from the inside-out! It's time for the world to see his mighty work in your lives," concluded Mama Timmons.

"If it weren't for this ministry and what God did through you, I—we would have died," said Amanda.

"Hey guys, do you remember when we first showed up here? On the wall, there were stations marked as Glass Only, Aluminum Only, Paper Products Only, Compost Products Only, Foam Products Only, Plastics Only, Clothing Only, Crayons Only, and a station that was marked OTHER," Tabitha said.

"How could we ever forget? It was a Sunday evening, the first day of summer," Chloe said.

"Mama Timmons said to each of us, find your stations on the wall and stay there until I finish with Officer Patterson. We looked at each other and thought she was crazy. I am not garbage, and how dare she think otherwise. We didn't understand back then, but now we do. We all stood at 'Other'! 'This lady didn't know who she was messing with,' we said to each other. If we band together, we will be out of here by morning. I guess the morning never came. But wait...it did, three and a half years later. That was the longest night ever."

"Yes, almost 1,185 days!" Isabella injected.

"Really, Isabella!" Courtney said.

"Y'all know that math is my thing."

THREE AND A HALF YEARS EARLIER...

"*T*hank you, Officer Patterson, don't worry, the girls will be fine with me," said Ms. Timmons.

"May God be with you, Ms. Timmons," replied Officer Patterson.

"He always is," Ms. Timmons said as she watched him drive off.

Ms. Timmons walked back into the house. "Okay, girls, as she looked at them piled up together. I see that you all have chosen 'Other.' Hmmm... okay, let's get you all assigned to a room."

"What? No explanation of what this all means!" shouted Tabitha.

Turning around, Ms. Timmons said in a small yet authoritative voice, "You will all understand by and by. But for now, room assignments, and then we will get washed up for dinner". With clipboard in hand, Mama Timmons began to make room assignments. "Tabitha and Paige, you are in Room #1. Lyric and Peyton, you are in Room #2. Isabella and Chloe, you are in Room #3. Courtney and Amanda, you are in Room #4. It is now 6:10 pm; meet me in the dining room at 6:30 pm."

The girls, with their bags in hand, hurried upstairs to find their rooms.

"THE ACQUAINTANCE"— LET'S GET TO KNOW YOU

(Room 1—Tabitha and Paige)

"Let's get one thing straight from the beginning," said Tabitha. "I don't know you. And, you don't know me. As far as I am concern, if you don't talk to me, I won't talk to you. I don't plan on being here long".

"If that's the way you want it, fine with me!" Paige snapped back at Tabitha.

(Room 2—Lyric and Peyton)

♪ "My name is Lyric! How are you?" ♪

"Is it necessary for you to sing your name?" Peyton said.

"It is for me. Singing makes me happy," Lyric said.

"So, what happens when the song stops?" Peyton asked.

Immediately, silence blanketed the room; a heavy garment of despair became its covering.

(Room 3—Isabella and Chloe)

"Why am I here? I am so sorry. I am so sorry. I am so sorry," Chloe repeatedly said as she sobbed.

"Stop crying, Chloe," Isabella said as she tried to console her. "What are you so sorry about?"

"You don't understand. I don't deserve to be here. I am just so sorry. So sorry."

(Room 4—Courtney and Amanda)

"Can I have the bed on this side of the room? I want to be close to the mirror," Courtney said.

"Oh, my goodness, please don't tell me that I am in the room with a "wanna-be-beauty-queen," Amanda responded.

"Excuse me, what did you say?"

"You heard me, a "wanna-be-beauty-queen.""

"You're just mad cause you don't look like me, with all of those gothic clothes." Courtney continues, "Why are you dressed like you are going to a funeral?"

"You don't know who you are messing with, girl. I will put some marks on you, but they won't be beautiful."

"Are you threatening me?"

"I never make threats."

"Ms. Timmons!" yelled Courtney as she ran down the stairs. "I demand to be moved out of this room."

"What is it, my dear?" Ms. Timmons responded.

"I demand that I change roommates!"

"Demand? Oh no, dear, we don't demand. Your placement is final until I tell you to move. Now, have a seat at the table and wait for the other girls to come while I go into the kitchen to bring dinner out. And, by the way, Courtney, her name is Amanda."

This woman is crazy, Courtney quietly said to herself. This woman is crazy. This situation is crazy. I am ready to go! But go where? I have no other place to go!

"What was all of that commotion going on?" some of the girls said as they came downstairs.

"Nothing for you all to concern yourselves. So, please, all of you have a seat at the table while I go get dinner out of the kitchen," Ms. Timmons said. The girls did as Ms. Timmons noted, with no one saying anything to each other.

Immediately, the crippling silence was interrupted by Tabitha. "Just so everyone knows, I don't plan on being here long, so don't anybody try to get to know me or talk to me."

"Honestly, what is with you? We've been here not even an hour, and you are already mouthing off; okay, we won't talk to you! Get over yourself!" Paige exclaimed!

Tabitha gets up, slams the chair under the table, and runs upstairs.

Ms. Timmons enters the dining room with dinner. She sets the table and sits down, noticing that Tabitha is not there. "Where is Tabitha, Paige?"

"I'm not Tabitha's keeper."

"Excuse me, young lady," Ms. Timmons said as she reprimanded Paige.

"I mean, I guess she went back to the room. She started mouthing off, saying that she didn't want anyone to talk to her or try to get to know her. So, I told her about herself," Paige growled.

"You told her about herself?" Ms. Timmons said puzzledly. "I didn't know the two of you knew each other."

"I don't know her. This is my first time seeing her," Paige replied.

"Oh, I see," Ms. Timmons responded. "So, you really didn't tell her about herself?" The room became still and quiet. The girls looked at each other, daring not to say a word. "Well, girls, we will not eat until Tabitha returns to the table," Ms. Timmons insisted. "Who's going to go and get her?"

A small voice broke the quiet-filled room, "I—I will go and get her Ms. Timmons if that's okay?"

"Thank you, Isabella," Ms. Timmons replied.

Isabella goes upstairs to get Tabitha. She knocks at the door. "Go away!" Tabitha yelled in anger!

"Umm, I can't do that," Isabella said. "Ms. Timmons said for me to come and get you, and I can't leave without you."

"Ughh, that woman," belted Tabitha. "What's up with her?"

"I think she may care about us," replied Isabella as Tabitha opened the door.

"What is your name," asks Tabitha?

"I'm Isabella. The food is getting cold, and I need you to come with me. We can't eat until all of us are at the table. I don't know about you, but I've been hungry before and had no clue how or if I would ever eat. You've already said that you don't want us to know you, but I need you to know me, I must eat now, and you must come with me."

Looking at Isabella, trying to seem unmoved by her story, Tabitha begrudgingly says, "Alright, alright, I will come down."

"Thank you, Tabitha."

When the girls came downstairs, Ms. Timmons welcomed Tabitha back, and they all sat down to eat. "Girls, first, we must say our Grace."

"Grace? I am hungry," Amanda yelled.

"I am too," Ms. Timmons said. "But we will say our Grace first. Do any of you want to say it?"

"I'll say it," Chloe said. "Lord, I'm sorry for being disobedient. I'm sorry for not doing what was right. Please bless this food and help us to be grateful. Amen."

To herself, Amanda begins to wonder... "What kind of prayer was that? Why would you tell God that you are sorry? What did she do to God?"

"Now, let's eat," Ms. Timmons said.

After dinner...

"Ms. Timmons, that food was so good!" Isabella said.

"Well, I'm glad that you girls enjoyed it."

Amanda got up from the table and looked at Ms. Timmons. "Thank you for dinner. I'm going to go and get settled in my room."

"Oh no, dear, not yet. You girls have some chores to do."

"Chores?

"That's right, chores. I cook, and you all will clean. I need Isabella and Chloe to remove the dirty dishes from the table and set it for breakfast in the morning. Lyric and Peyton will sweep and mop. Courtney and Amanda, you will wash and dry the dishes."

"That means we are free," Tabitha said. "I'm going to bed!"

Tabitha and Paige, come with me, Ms. Timmons said.

"Where are we going?" Paige asked. "There's nothing left for us to do."

"There's always something for you to do," Ms. Timmons said.

In the laundry room...

The girls follow Ms. Timmons to the laundry room. "Okay, girls, I need you to put two sets of towels in each of your rooms. A towel set will consist of a bath and a hand towel, and a washcloth. Make sure you put a set on each of the girls' beds. Once you finish with the rooms, stock the two linen closets upstairs with the remaining towels and washcloths. Each cabinet is labeled and in order. Make sure you keep them that way."

"Yes, ma'am," said Paige. "I have never seen so many towels." Ms. Timmons laughs and walks away.

"Who does this woman think she is? We are not slaves!" exclaimed Tabitha. "I am so out of here."

"I have had it up to here with your mouth, and again, we've not been here very long. So, just shut up and do as you are told," Paige said with authority.

"Girl, you don't know me," exclaimed Tabitha.

"And according to you, I never will, so get the towels, and let's go," replied Paige.

In the kitchen...

"I am going to mess my nails up washing these dishes," whines Courtney.

"Oh, my goodness, listen, let's set the record straight," Amanda says. "I told you earlier that you are not all that! And you are not so delicate that you can't wash these dishes." Amanda walks over and grabs Courtney's hands and shoves them in the water.

"What are you doing? Oh no, yells Courtney!"

"Now, what are you going to do about that," Amanda said, laughing as the water and suds splashed everywhere. Courtney quickly shielded her face from the splashing water.

"Ms. Timmons, Ms. Timmons!" yelled Courtney.

Hurriedly walking to the kitchen, "What is it, Courtney"? says Ms. Timmons.

"Amanda made me broke a nail!"

"And how did she do that, asks Ms. Timmons?

"She shoved my hands."

Amanda interrupts. "I got tired of her complaining about not wanting to wash dishes. She must think she's a queen."

"Amanda!" Ms. Timmons said with displeasure.

"I know I shouldn't have done that, Ms. Timmons, and I am sorry."

"You girls have to learn to have more patience with each other."

"You want me to have patience with her, Ms. Timmons," Amanda asked reluctantly?

"Her?"

"I'm sorry; you want me to have patience with Courtney?"

"Yes, my dear, patience. Now, I need you girls to get this water dried up from the floor and finish the dishes. Any questions?"

"No ma'am, Ms. Timmons," said Courtney, "and I am sorry also."

"You don't need to apologize to me, but to each other."

"I'm sorry, Amanda; I will do my part in cleaning."

"I am sorry too. I didn't mean to break your nail Courtney," responded Amanda.

In the dining room...

As Isabella cleans the plates, she stashes food away in her pockets. Unbeknown to her, Chloe sees her but never says a word. "We're almost done in here. All we have to do now is wipe the table down and set the dishes for breakfast. I will take the dirty dishes to the kitchen," said Chloe.

"Okay, I will take the breakfast dishes out of the cupboard," said Isabella.

While waiting to sweep and mop...

♪I'm going to mop, and you're going to sweep, la la la la! You're going to sweep, and I'm going to mop, la la la la! ♪ "Sing it with me, Peyton."

"Would you stop already! I am not going to sing with you," said Peyton.

"You're such a pooper," said Lyric. "One of these days, your music is going to stop," Peyton said very spitefully.

"No, please don't say that! It can't!" Covering her ears, hysterically exclaiming, I can't hear you and singing her song louder and louder. ♪♪♪

After the girls finished their chores...

"Thank you, girls, you did an excellent job," said Ms. Timmons.

"Can we go to our rooms now," Amanda asked? "I am so sleepy."

"Just a minute; you girls will need to be dressed and ready for breakfast by 8 am tomorrow," Ms. Timmons said. "Tabitha and Paige have put clean towel sets in each of your rooms. There are two full baths upstairs and one half-bath. For Rooms 1 and 2, you will get the Bathroom Escape, and for rooms 3 and 4, you will get Bathroom Peace. The names are on the doors."

"What strange labels for bathrooms?" Peyton thought.

"You will be responsible for keeping the bathrooms clean," Ms. Timmons continued.

"And girls, give us a chance. I know this is your first night here, and you have a lot of mixed emotions right now, but I give you my word if you let yourself be, everything will work out." The girls dropped their heads as Ms. Timmons continued to talk. "I hope you have a good night!"

"Good night Ms. Timmons," the girls responded as they rushed upstairs.

Room 3

"Isabella, can I ask you a question?"

"Of course, what's up, Chloe?" she responded as she got her things ready for the shower.

"I saw you putting food away in your pockets while we were cleaning."

"What?! You were spying on me?"

"No, no, it's not like that. Calm down."

"Now, you are going to go and blab your mouth."

"No, Isabella, I won't."

"How can I trust you?"

"I don't know. You just have to. Remember, earlier before dinner, when you were trying to console me. I just want to return your kindness."

"Have you ever been hungry?" Isabella asked Chloe. "I mean, really, hungry."

"Well," Chloe started.

Abruptly interrupted by Isabella, "don't answer Chloe because you haven't." "I don't want you to think that I am a bad person because I stole that food tonight. I'm so used to storing food for the next day out of fear that I wouldn't eat. I'm not a bad person, or at least I didn't start that way."

(There's a knock at the door.) "Who is it?" Chloe responds to the knock at the door.

It's us, Room 4—Courtney and Amanda.

"Give me a second, please," whispered Isabella to Chloe.

"Okay, we're coming," exclaimed Chloe! (At the door and looking back at Isabella) "Are you okay?"

"Yes, let them in.

(Chloe opens the door) "Hey, y'all. Come on in."

"We felt like we should talk about our bathroom assignment since we will be sharing, asserted Courtney.

"Okay," said Isabella and Chloe.

"I can't stand a nasty bathroom," blurted Amanda. "So, we must keep it clean. When a person finishes, they are responsible for cleaning up their mess and preparing it for the next person. I think we should each get thirty minutes of uninterrupted bathroom time in the morning and at night. Does everyone agree?"

"Yes," the girls said in unison.

"We need a schedule," says Isabella. "Okay, let's make one."

Room 1

"I have one question for you Tabitha, what is your problem, and why are you so hateful? Paige said in disgust.

"I think that's two questions. I guess you can't count," Tabitha retaliated.

"Whatever, girl! You are a very bitter person," shouted Paige.

"Look, I told you before, I don't want you to know me, and I'm not going to try to know you or any of you for that matter," warned Tabitha. "I've been in and out of these kinds of places, so I know the ropes. I'm here only to do enough to make my time pass before I am shipped out again."

"So, that's why you are so angry," uttered Paige.

"But listen, I am not ANGRY! THIS IS THE LIFE I HAVE GOTTEN USED TO! I HAVE TO GET YOU BEFORE YOU GET ME!"

"I feel sorry for you, Tabitha!"

"Don't feel sorry for me. You should feel sorry for yourself." (Tabitha walks out and slams the door.)

Downstairs

"Now, who is that slamming my door? Girls, are you all okay up there," called Ms. Timmons?

Yes, Ms. Timmons. "Rooms 3 and 4 are good."

♪ "We are too," sings Lyric.

"Ms. Timmons, it was Tabitha. She and I had some words, and she walked out," confessed Paige.

"Where is she now?"

"She locked herself in the bathroom."

Ms. Timmons walks upstairs. "The rest of you girls, finish up and get yourselves ready for bed." (Ms. Timmons knocks on the door of Bathroom Escape) "Tabitha. Come on, sweetheart, open the door."

"I don't want to, Ms. Timmons; please just leave me alone."

"I can't do that, baby girl. So, open the door, or I will use my key." (The lock turns on the door, and Tabitha walks out.) With her hand extended to Tabitha, come with me to my room, says Ms. Timmons. (The two depart downstairs.)

Room #2

"I just love taking showers. So, while the coast is clear, I will run in," says Lyric.

(♪ A beautiful song fills the upstairs, and the girls start coming out of their rooms.) Who's that singing?

"It's Lyric," said Peyton. She's always singing.

"Lyric has a beautiful voice, said Paige.

"Okay, but why does she have to sing everything all the time?" Peyton asked.

"I don't know, but if I had a voice like that, I would be singing all the time too," said Courtney.

"Her voice is like light pouring into darkness," Amanda said.

"I feel a weird sense of peace," said Isabella.

"Yea, like everything, is going to be alright," Chloe said as she looked at Isabella.

(The girls go back to their assigned rooms.)

Downstairs in Ms. Timmons Room

"Come on in and sit down on the chair. Now, tell me what's wrong," Ms. Timmons asked Tabitha.

"Nothing is wrong with me. I just wish everyone would just leave me alone. These girls don't care about me anyway. No one ever has, she murmured."

"Now, don't say that."

"But it's true. You don't know my story, Ms. Timmons."

"And you don't know mine, Tabitha."

"Yea, you probably grew up with the perfect family."

"It's all according to your definition of perfect. Listen Tabitha, I know you are hurting, confused, and filled with rage and anger inside. You are a volcano on the verge of an explosion. I want to help you, my dear. Let us help you."

Crying, Tabitha explains to Ms. Timmons, "Can't you see; no one can help me! My life is messy! Nothing good lives inside of me!"

Embracing Tabitha, Ms. Timmons, in a tender voice, says, "You can't see her now, but you will one day."

"See who? I don't understand," Ms. Timmons.

"I know you don't know, but you will. Come on, get yourself cleaned up, go and shower and get some rest. We have a big day tomorrow."

(Leaving the room, Tabitha turns around) "Thank you, Ms. Timmons."

"You are most welcome, my dear, now off to bed."

"Yes ma'am."

Ms. Timmons follows Tabitha upstairs and knocks on each of their doors. "Girls, I need you all to come out in the hall a moment."

"What's wrong, Ms. Timmons? Did we do something wrong?" asks Peyton.

"I called you out, so we could pray.

"Pray?"

"Yes, pray. We must say our prayers every night before going to bed."

"Umm, Ms. Timmons, do you think God still hears us even though we messed up? I want him to forgive me. I didn't mean to hurt anyone," says Chloe.

"You said that during dinner, Chloe. What does it all mean?" asks Amanda.

"I—I—I, maybe later Amanda," said Chloe.

Ms. Timmons leads the girls in prayer, and afterward, they depart to their rooms.

The next day...

(Around 6 am, Isabella comes downstairs, fully dressed) "Isabella, what are you doing up so early," said Ms. Timmons.

"I thought you could use some help with fixing breakfast," she replied. "I liked cooking at one time, but..."

"But what dear?"

"I don't want to talk about it."

"Okay, in your time, just know I am here for you. Would you like to scramble the eggs for me?"

"Yes ma'am!"

"You can go ahead and get them prepared, but we won't scramble them until 7:30 am.

"Okay." (While cracking the eggs) "Ms. Timmons, I'm a little confused about something.

What is it, dear? What's the meaning of the stations on the wall? And why did you tell us to find our stations?

Do you, well, I mean, do you think we are trash, Ms. Timmons?"

(Ms. Timmons stops what she is doing and walks over to Isabella.) "You are not trash, but I believe that some things inside each of you must be discarded and destroyed just like trash, so you can be the beautiful person I know who lives inside you."

"You mean, you think that I have some beauty inside of me? How can that be? I'm here because of all the ugly things that I have done or forced to do," she said under her breath.

"Isabella, God, can take all your ugly and make it beautiful!"

(Chloe enters the room) "There you are I was looking for you, Isabella. Good morning Ms. Timmons!"

"Good morning dear! Did you rest well?"

"Yes, ma'am." (Turning to Isabella) "I was worried about you. At my last home, we had a girl who was a runner. And, I thought maybe, you…"

Interrupting Chloe, Isabella quickly said, "No, I didn't run away. I came down early to help Ms. Timmons with breakfast."

"Oh my, look at the time," Ms. Timmons said as she hurriedly prepared the last dishes for breakfast. "It's 7:30am, and we've got to get breakfast on the table. Isabella, start frying the eggs. Chloe, get the milk and orange juice out of the refrigerator and put them on the table. I will place the food in the serving bowls and dishes."

(Breakfast is on the table, and all the girls are down-stairs waiting for Ms. Timmons to give the okay to come to the table.)

"Good morning Princesses!" (The girls are stunned by what Ms. Timmons said and frozen in movement) "You may come to the table and be seated."

"Did she just call us princesses?" Paige whispered.

"Shhh...I don't get this lady," Courtney replied.

"Are you all coming to the table? You aren't hungry?" Ms. Timmons inquired.

"Oh yes, ma'am! I am starving," said Isabella. (The girls cautiously walked to the table where they are seated.)

"Who would like to say the Grace?"

"Can I say it, Ms. Timmons?" Lyric exclaimed. "It's actually a song that my grandma taught me when I was younger."

"Go right ahead!"

Lyric started singing...

♪*God our Father,*
God our Father,
We Thank You,
We Thank You,
For Your Many Blessings,
For Your Many Blessings,
Amen, Amen! ♪

"Amen!" The girls said as they began eating.

"Ms. Timmons, what are we going to do today?" Tabitha asked.

"Yea, you said we have a big day today," Courtney chimed in.

"But first things first girls, let's finish eating before the food gets cold. Then I will give you the Agenda for today."

(Breakfast is over and Ms. Timmons assign the morning chores.) "Tabitha and Paige, you will wash the dishes. Lyric and Peyton, you will clean the table and set it up for lunch. Courtney and Amanda, you will sweep. Chloe and Isabella, you get to rest for an hour since you girls helped with preparing breakfast. Girls let's meet in the den at 10 am. That gives you an hour to get your chores done and rest for a moment."

"Yes ma'am," they replied as they started their chores.

"Isabella, would you like to finish our conversation from last night?" Chloe asked.

"Um, I guess so—where did we leave off?"

"You were asking me if I ever was hungry..."

"Oh yes. When I was younger, I had the perfect family until tragedy came knocking at our door one day."

"What happened?"

"My mom and dad brought my siblings and me into the den and sat us down, and they told us that we were not going to be a family anymore. My siblings and I looked at each other in disbelief and confusion. Being the oldest and a daddy's girl, I looked at my mom and started screaming at her...what did you do to my dad? She walked away crying, and my dad came to me and said that it wasn't your mom, it was me. You, dad? What do you mean?" His response was, 'I no longer want to be a part of this family.' He grabbed his things, and that was the last time that I ever saw him. My mom did everything she could to raise me and my sister and brother. Night after night, I heard her cry. She had to work two jobs just to make ends meet and keep food on the table. Some days we went without seeing my mom. We were hungry and constantly living in fear that she would leave us too.

"Isabella, I am so sorry. But how did you end up here?"

"I had to feed my brother and sister. Although my mom was trying her best... her monies went to keeping a roof over our heads. She had to make a choice...food or a place to stay? I started hanging out at restaurants waiting for them to throw out food that they could not use and bakeries as they threw out day-old pastries and bread. I got enough to fill the bellies of my siblings and me. Every day, I patiently waited outside their doors to retrieve what I could. One day the owner of one of the bakeries saw me going through the trash to get the bread, and she threatened to call the police if I returned.

"Do you mean she didn't even ask you what was wrong? It was already in the trash."

"You're right, Chloe, but that's not how it works. I couldn't let this stop me, though; I just had to be more careful next time. This food search went on for months. I thought I was outsmarting everyone until the cops were waiting for me at the restaurant one day. I outsmarted the baker but fell into a trap at the restaurant. The police ordered a DSS home inspection because of my actions, and just like that, we were taken away from my mother. Each of us ended up in a different home. It was only supposed to be temporary until my mom got herself together. Temporary arrangements turned into a year. Since then, I've been from one foster home to the next. I don't know what's going on with my little brother and sister. The last home I was in, they didn't let me talk to them. It's all my fault, as she started to cry. If it weren't for me, we would still be together.

Chloe extends her hand to Isabella. "We all have a lot that we are sorry for, but I feel like this place is different from other residential homes. I just believe that both of us are going to get the help we need, Isabella."

"How can you be so sure, Chloe?"

"I can't explain it, but Ms. Timmons is different, and I bet you if you told her what happened, she would help you.

"Girls," Ms. Timmons called.

"You better get cleaned up."

"Yes Ms. Timmons, we are coming."

(Chloe and Isabella walk inside)

"Okay, girls, now that morning chores are done, I need to speak with all of you." (The girls all walk into the den.) "Do you see the stations on the wall?"

"Yes, but Ms. Timmons, this is not right. I am not trash!" Tabitha exclaims!

"She's right. We are not trash," Paige answered.

"Well, the two of you finally agreed on something," Ms. Timmons said.

"She thinks we are trash just like everyone else," Courtney cried.

Lyric raises her hand. "Yes, Lyric," Ms. Timmons said as she recognized her hand.

"Please help me to understand what you are telling me. Are you saying that we are trash? If so, it doesn't make me feel good inside."

"What, no song?" Peyton said laughing.

"Girls, girls, calm down. I have a project for you. There are eight stations with signs on the wall…"

"Ms. Timmons, you forgot about the one station that says Other," interrupted Chloe.

"Yes, you are right, but let me finish."

"I'm sorry, Ms. Timmons."

Ms. Timmons continued, "I am assigning each of you a station. You will do a research paper on the recycling process for each item."

"What kind of project is that?" Amanda murmured. "First, she wanted us to pick a station like we were trash, now she wants us to write about recycling. This lady is strange."

Ignoring what Amanda said, Ms. Timmons continued. "I will give you all until Saturday, after lunch, to have it completed. Then, each of you will present your station to the group after we are done eating."

Ms. Timmons hands out the assignments, and the girls quickly ran upstairs. "I will see you all at 12:30 pm for lunch. One last thing, Ms. Timmons shouted upstairs, "do not share your topics. We will find out together what everyone has."

Room #1

"You know it felt kind of weird that you and I agreed on something, don't you think, Tabitha?"

"Maybe, but I.."

Interrupting Tabitha, Paige says sarcastically, "I know, I know...you don't have to say it...you don't want to know me. It was just an observation, that's all, you don't have to get upset."

Room #2

"What happened to you down there? Since we got here, all you ever do is sing, but your song left when we thought Ms. Timmons called us trash," Peyton commented.

"Why do you care? You wanted me to stop singing, remember, you said my song would stop one day," Lyric whimpered.

"I'm sorry, Lyric; I shouldn't have said that. It was petty of me."

"Apology accepted," Lyric said. "I started to have flashbacks from a miserable time in my life. You see, that's all I've ever been called and compared to...TRASH! I'm never going to be anything because I am nothing, and I came from nothing. So, Peyton, tell me, where is the song in that? It's kind of hard to believe otherwise when you are told that all your life."

"If you're nothing, that means I'm nothing, and two nothings can't be talking to each other right now," Peyton said. The girls share a laugh through their hidden pain.

Room #3

"Isabella, have you ever been to church before?"

"I have a few times. Sometimes, I went with my foster parents, but never before then."

"What about you, Chloe?"

"I used to go all the time. The church was peaceful for me."

"Then, I don't understand, Chloe. How did you end up here?"

"I made a terrible decision that cost my best friend her life," Chloe says as the tears began rolling down her face as if someone had turned on a water faucet.

Room #4

"This project is a very peculiar yet intriguing assignment. What do you have, Amanda?"

"Didn't you hear Ms. Timmons? We cannot reveal until Saturday."

"You're right. I like doing projects."

"That's because you are a project yourself," Amanda said, speaking under her breath about Courtney.

"What's that?" Courtney inquired.

"O, nothing. I think I'm going to take a nap before lunch."

"You go right ahead. I'm starting our assignment," said Courtney.

After Lunch

Lunchtime has come and gone, and the girls are all in the den watching TV, waiting for Ms. Timmons. "May I ask everyone a question," says Courtney?

"It depends on what it is," Tabitha spouts off.

"I am so sick of you, what is your problem? Why are you so mean?" Paige asked.

"Hey guys, calm down," Isabella intervenes. "We are going to get in trouble."

"Not we, it's her," yelled Paige!

"Courtney, please go ahead and ask your question," Chloe said.

"I was just wondering if any of you have started your projects. I have, and I honestly didn't know how I could learn so much about the 'ugly me' from, I hate to say it... TRASH!"

"What do you mean," Lyric said?

"All I can say is take your part seriously and be open."

"How were you able to start researching so fast? Ms. Timmons took our phones when we came here last night," Amanda asked.

"I know, but I went and told her that I wanted to get started on my project, and guess what? She has a computer lab in the basement that we can use for school."

"School? I'm not planning on being here the whole summer," Tabitha shouted.

"Here she goes again. Shut up, Tabitha!" Paige says as Ms. Timmons walks in.

"Oh, no ma'am. We don't use language like that."

"But Ms. Timmons, you just don't know. This girl is hateful for no reason."

"Paige, don't be so quick to react. Learn to sit back and observe."

"So, you are condoning her rude behavior, Ms. Timmons."

"No, Princess, I do not agree with her actions, but I don't agree with yours either. Just because she is wrong doesn't make it okay for you to be inappropriate, also."

On the other side of the room, thinking to herself, Peyton says, "Ms. Timmons called her a Princess. Does she not see who we are? I don't understand this lady!"

"You sound just like the officer who arrested me. He said the same thing to me. I'm sorry, Ms. Timmons."

"I forgive you," Paige.

"I guess I am, too," Tabitha said reluctantly.

"Hmmm, you think," said Ms. Timmons.

"I mean, I am sorry, Ms. Timmons."

"Not to me, my dear, but to the girls."

Tabitha looks over at the girls and quickly said, "Sorry."

"Now, what were you girls talking about," Ms. Timmons asks.

"I was telling them about the computer lab," said Courtney.

"Oh yes, girls. Let's do a tour of the house. In each room, you will find instructions on how to use the space properly."

The girls follow Ms. Timmons, but Peyton, still deep in her thoughts, lags. "I wish I could see as Ms. Timmons, but my vision is so dark and scarred with the ugly I've done. Will Princess be a title for me someday?" In the background of her thoughts, she hears Lyric singing her name...

♪"Peyton, where are you?"

"I'm coming," she responded.

Ms. Timmons continues, "Girls, we will start in the basement and then move upstairs. Here's the computer lab that

Courtney told you all about. The lab is open at certain times during the day. See the schedule on the door. Each of you will be assigned a new laptop. Each laptop comes with security features that prohibit the viewing of certain websites. I will get an alarm if you try to go around the security features."

"What if we need to use the computer lab outside of the posted hours?" Paige asked.

"All you have to do is let me know, and I will open it for you. The next room is the game room/theatre."

"Wow, this is a huge room? What are those smaller rooms, Ms. Timmons?" Isabella asked.

"Those are called prayer closets."

"Prayer closets?"

"Yes, lots of prayers have gone up in those closets over the years."

"What if we don't know how to pray," quietly asked Tabitha?

"Don't worry, you will learn. God, through me, will teach you." "There's a full bathroom over there."

"What's its name?" Paige asked?

"Look at the door."

"On the sign, it reads, Bathroom Peace. Ms. Timmons, why did you choose these names?"

Looking at Paige, her only answer is a smile.

Ms. Timmons continues touring the girls through the house. "Okay, that's all down here; let's go back to the main floor. You are familiar with everything up here, except for the laundry room. Here it is on your left. Please see the laundry room schedule on the door. Everyone is responsible for washing their clothes. All clothes will be washed, dried, folded, and ironed, if necessary. Wash days will begin on Friday and end on Saturdays. I will discard clothes left in the dryer."

With her eyes stretched in disbelief, "You mean you will throw them in the trash?" Chloe asked.

"Yes, I will. People who want their things are careful not to lose them."

"Do you think she's serious?" whispered Amanda.

"I don't want to find out, so we better do as she says. There's something about Ms. Timmons that I just can't figure out," Courtney noted. "Do you girls have any questions?" asked Ms. Timmons.

"No, ma'am," they said.

"Okay, I would like you girls to set your rooms up how you want them and start your research projects." (The girls go upstairs)

Room #2

Peyton begins looking at herself in the mirror as if she had x-ray vision.

"What's wrong Peyton?" Lyric asked. "Why are you looking at yourself as if you've never seen yourself before?"

"Ms. Timmons called Paige a Princess," Peyton responded. "Do you think she really saw a Princess in Paige? And do you think she can see a Princess in me too?"

"I don't think Ms. Timmons would lie," Lyric said as she shrugged her shoulders. "I want to see the Princess in me, but there is so much blocking my view." Peyton continues, "All I see is what I've done and what I've been through in my life."

Not paying Peyton any attention, Lyric interrupts. "Come on, Peyton, we've got to get this room set up."

Peyton, troubled in mind, walks away from the mirror to help Lyric with the room.

Room #1

"Okay Paige," saying to herself, "take a deep breath before you go into this room. Remember what Ms. Timmons said, stop being so quick to react, but take time to observe." Opening the door to the room, Paige walks in and sees Tabitha sitting on the bed. "Hey Tabitha. Are you ready to start decorating our room?"

"I don't know why we are setting up this room. I'm not going to be here for long." Looking for a fight from Paige, Tabitha continues to hurl out negative comments, but Paige sits patiently, not saying a word. What's wrong with her, thought Tabitha? "Did you hear me, Paige?"

"Yes, I did. I felt that if we moved the beds this way, we would each have more room. What do you think, Tabitha?"

"I already told you I'm not going to be here long," Tabitha responded.

"I know, but can you help me move this around."

"You aren't going to get me to help you do anything," Tabitha says.

"It's okay, but can you get this and put it over there, and bring that to me, and..."

Before Tabitha knew it, the whole room had been re-arranged. Thinking to herself, "Did I just help this girl?"

"Thanks for your help, Tabitha. I'm going downstairs to work on the project."

"Don't say anything to me!" Tabitha bellowed.

With a smile, Paige walks out of the room with her stuff in hand. On the other side of the door, she takes a deep breath. "It worked! It worked! I've got to tell Ms. Timmons."

Room #3

"Can you believe Ms. Timmons has prayer closets in her house?" asked Isabella. "Here is our chance to make things right."

"Yes!" sighs Chloe. "I don't know if God will forgive me for what I did."

"You were telling me earlier that you made a wrong decision that cost your friend's life. What happened, Chloe?"

"My parents allowed me to drive to the store by myself for the first time. They told me to go straight there and back, but I didn't. I called my best friend Tonya and went to her house. She got in the car, and we were on our way, laughing and talking to the store. I got what I wanted, and as we were on our way back, I got a text message, and I answered it. I lost control of the car and ended up going off the road, hitting a ditch. The vehicle flipped multiple times. Tonya was ejected from the vehicle. I was unconscious and awoke in the hospital to many bright lights and hearing what sounded like my mother crying. I was so confused. I called for Tonya, but she never answered. All I heard was a lot of noise and crying and talking. Before I knew it, I was out again. Some time passed, and I awoke to my mom and dad standing over me. I remember saying, Mom, dad...where am I? Where is Tonya? At that moment, my dad said, 'there was an accident and Princess, I am so sorry, but the car accident killed Tonya.' I began screaming and crying uncontrollably."

••

"My best friend, DEAD! This can't be real, and I caused it! From that point, I spun out of control. My parents sought counseling for me, they tried to help me, but I couldn't forgive myself. I wanted to die, too! Several failed attempts at suicide. Several placements in various facilities. Trying to fill my guilt with different things, I ended up deeper and deeper in trouble.

What possessed me to defy my parents? I always did what they told me. Tonya is dead over a stupid text message! I killed her...I killed her. Tell me, Isabella, how do you recover from that? Chloe drops her head in Isabella's lap as she cries uncontrollably.

••

"I don't know Chloe," Isabella responds with compassion. "However, I just feel like the answer will be in those prayer closets."

••

Room #4

"Courtney, I think we did a great job. The room looks good. Are you ready to go downstairs to work on our projects?" Amanda asks.

"Yes, let's go, Courtney tells Amanda. As the girls walk to the computer lab, they engage in conversation.

"Amanda, remember, when you start your project, you have to start with an open mind."

"Courtney, we're talking about trash here. There's not much you can get out of waste."

"You'll see. Wait until you start on your questions."

Computer Lab

The door opens, and Paige is startled. "We didn't mean to frighten you, says Amanda."

"Oh, no problem, it's a spooky down here when you are by yourself," Paige said.

"Yeah, you're right," Courtney answered. "That's how I felt earlier when I was here by myself."

"Your name is Courtney, right?"

"Yes, and this is my roommate Amanda."

"I am Paige."

"Yes, we remember. Where is Tabitha?"

"She's upstairs. Hopefully, she will be down soon. But I don't know."

"That was some excellent advice that Ms. Timmons gave earlier on how to deal with her."

"Who, Tabitha?"

"Yes. She is a very bitter girl," Amanda chimes in.

Surprisingly, Paige begins to defend Tabitha. "She has a lot of anger inside her, but I believe that she will get better just like the rest of us."

"If you say so," Amanda said as she shook her head in doubt.

At the door of the Prayer Closet (start here)

"Are you going to go inside, Chloe?" Isabella asked.

"I don't know. Those two rooms are extraordinary, Isabella."

"Exactly! That's why I believe that your answer is inside."

"And what about your own solution? Chloe responded.

"I'm not talking about me," Isabella said in frustration. "We are talking about you." Isabella continues, "My answer may be in there as well, but I'm not the one that's constantly crying and saying sorry all the time. Although I just met you, I want you to be better. Are you ready to go inside the computer lab to get our projects done?"

"You can go on ahead. I'll be there in a minute, Chloe replied."

Isabella walks away, hoping that she didn't offend her roommate.

Chloe, with her back against the wall, begins to slide to the floor, talking to herself. "God, I don't understand! How did I get here? I had it all together and one stupid mistake, and I have lost everything." Suddenly the door to one of the prayer closets opens, and Ms. Timmons comes out. "You know, it's much better inside than out here in the hallway," Ms. Timmons whispered.

"Ms. Timmons, you scared me."

"Oh, I didn't mean to scare you, dear. Are you okay, Chloe?"

"Umm, oh yes, ma'am! Yes, ma'am, I am," as she says, getting up from the floor.

"Would you like to go in?"

"Not now, Ms. Timmons, I have to get to the computer lab. I will see you later!" she said as she hurriedly walked away.

"God, in your perfect timing, I will patiently," Ms. Timmons says as she watches Chloe walks down the hall.

In the Computer Lab

"Hey, Y'all!" Chloe said as she walked in the Computer Lab.

I was beginning to get worried about you. I thought you were right behind me," Isabella said.

"I just needed to stay put for a while," responded Chloe.

"Well, did you go into the prayer room, Chloe?"

"No, but guess who came out of the second closet?"

"Who? Who?"

"Ms. Timmons. She tried to get me to go in, but I just couldn't. I wanted to, but I couldn't. So, she stayed and talked with me in the hall." "So, where do we begin?" Chloe said trying to change subjects.

"We must follow the guidelines on this paper," explained Courtney as she walked over towards Chloe and Isabella. See, your laptop is here."

"How did you know that?" asked Chloe.

"Uhhh...your name is on it, silly." The girls all laughed as they started to work individually on their assignments.

The door opens. Peyton and Lyric walk in. Hey guys! Hey, y'all!

"I was wondering where you all were," said Amanda. "We just got finished with our room. What should we do now?"

"Over here. I will show you," said Courtney. "Each one of us has a laptop and workstation. Peyton, here's yours, and Lyric, you're right here."

"How did you know all this stuff?"

"Oh, please let me answer," interrupted Chloe. "Your names are on the laptops, silly!" All the girls begin to laugh.

Peyton and Lyric look at each other puzzledly. "Did we miss something?"

"Just before you walked in, Chloe asked the very same question," said Courtney. Peyton and Lyric laugh.

"Here are the questions for the project."

"Thank you, Courtney."

"If any of you have any questions or problems with your laptops, just let me know. I'm good at working with technology." Courtney walks back over to her workstation and continues to work on her project.

Sitting at her station, Paige watches the door, hoping Tabitha would soon come in, but she never does.

Upstairs in the Den

"Ms. Timmons," Tabitha said in a whiny and whispery voice. Not hearing Tabitha, Ms. Timmons continues reading her bible. Tabitha walks closer to Ms. Timmons and gently places her hand on her shoulders, calling her name again. "Ms. Timmons."

"Tabitha?" Ms. Timmons was startled by her presence at first. "I didn't hear you come in. I was preparing for your presentations. By the way, why aren't you in the computer lab with the other girls? What happened? Was there another blow-up?"

"No ma'am, I just can't...I just can't."

"What can't you do, sweetheart?"

Tabitha defeatedly sits on the sofa with tears running from her eyes. "I can't read well. The letters and the words all seem to run together."

"So, that's the reason for so much anger?"

"Ms. Timmons, I didn't have a childhood. I remember when I was in first grade, I couldn't go to school like other kids. Instead, I was home waiting for my mom to come home to feed us, or better yet, my brothers and sisters had to go outside and bring her in because she fell asleep on the porch. After all, she was too drunk to find the doorknob. This dysfunction was my life! Day after day! So, yes, I am angry because I missed the years in school where I should have been learning. Instead, I was busy taking care of a woman who was supposed to be taking care of my siblings and me. My other family members knew what was going on, but they did nothing to help us! I hate all of them, Ms. Timmons because they chose to let us die instead of rescuing us. By the time the courts did anything about it, I was already in 3rd grade and had already missed so much. I wanted to learn. I even stole the books from school to teach myself how to read and do the math and other stuff, but tell me Ms. Timmons, how was I, an uneducated third grader, supposed to instruct myself?

"I am so sorry, Tabitha."

"I don't want your pity, Ms. Timmons!" snaps Tabitha.

"Okay, pity, I will not give. But you can't give yourself pity either. If you genuinely want to do something about your reading, you will have to put forth some extra work."

"I want to learn! I don't want to be stupid."

Pausing a moment and tasting every word before she utters, Ms. Timmons responded, "Now Tabitha, first things first. I will not have you or any of my girls using words like stupid or any other derogatory terms describing yourself or each other or any other person in or away from my presence. I know you are angry. I know you are hurt. I know you don't understand genuine compassion when you see it. But let's get one thing straight, for you to heal, you will have to lose the attitude, my dear! You won't make it in life that way. I just met you two days ago, physically, but I've known you for a while."

"What do you mean by that, Ms. Timmons?"

"You will find out soon enough."

"You keep saying that. What will I find out?"

"Never mind that for now. There's a matter of your project assignment that we must work to find a solution. Yes ma'am. After dinner tonight, we will begin working."

"What about the other girls? I don't want them to know my business."

"Are you going to let your pride stop you from being the best person you can be? All of you have stories. It's called life. And no life outweighs the other. There's a choice that you need to make! If you want help, meet me in the computer lab after you finish your dinner chores."

BACK TO THE GRADUATION DINNER (PRESENT-DAY)

"Mama Timmons, a whole new world opened for me that night," Tabitha reflected. "I was finally able to learn. I didn't understand it then, but my STUBBORNNESS and REBELLIOUS attitude was going to KILL me."

"But it didn't, extending her hand to Tabitha," Paige said. You are VALEDICTORIAN and my BEST FRIEND! Satan had it designed for none of us to LIVE! He wanted to kill us physically and spiritually."

"Mama Timmons, I'm still amazed when I think about how God used you to make us do a project on recycling trash," Peyton said.

Girl, Recycled!

"I believe that Saturday when we made our presentations, the initial separation of our old selves began," Courtney injected. "Remember..."

BACK TO THE RECYCLING PRESENTATIONS

Friday Evening—In Chloe's and Isabella's Room

"*I* am so nervous, Chloe!" said Isabella.

"Nervous about what?"

"Our presentations will begin after our morning chores tomorrow."

"Have you forgotten Chloe?"

"Of course not, but I'm not scared." Suddenly, there's a knock at the door. "I wonder..." The door immediately opens.

"You don't have to wonder anymore," Amanda said as she came walking through the door. "Hey, Y'all!"

"Hey Amanda. Hey Courtney."

"I just wanted to check to see if you guys were ready for tomorrow."

"Yes, but I'm nervous."

"Me too!"

Lyric and Peyton walk-in. "What's up? We heard voices, so we came down."

"Come on in. We were just talking about the presentation tomorrow."

"I have been thinking about that since dinner," Peyton said.

"Hey, what's going on?"

"Oh, hey Paige. We were just talking about tomorrow. Come on in. We have plenty of floor and bed space for all of us to sit," Chloe said.

"Paige, where's Tabitha?" asks Amanda.

"I think she is with Ms. Timmons. She sure has been spending a lot of time with Ms. Timmons lately."

"I know, right. But let me just tell you, her attitude has been a whole lot better."

"Did I hear my name being called?

Startled, Paige responds, "yes, we were just wondering where you were."

"Why are all of you down here?" Tabitha asks.

"We are just talking about tomorrow and our presentations."

"Yes, we have a BIG day tomorrow. I'm going to get washed up and ready for bed. Good night, everyone!"

"Good night, Tabitha, the girls responded.

"Wow! Was that Tabitha?"

"Yes, it was. Tabitha has the right idea. I'm going to bed. Good night," Amanda said.

All the girls departed to their rooms.

Room #2

"Peyton, Peyton, wake up."

"What is it? What's wrong, Lyric?"

"Ever since we got here, Ms. Timmons has been coming up and praying with us before bed, but tonight she didn't. I think she is setting us up."

"Setting us up?! What do you mean, girl?"

"I believe this is part of the presentation tomorrow. She wants to see what we are going to do. I'm going to wake everyone, so we can gather in the hall to pray. Come on, you go to Courtney and Amanda, and I'll get everyone else."

The girls depart, knocking on the doors of the other girls, gathering them to meet in the hall. Finally, they are all there. "Lyric, what's going on; why did you wake us up?" Paige groaned.

"We didn't pray. Ms. Timmons has been gathering us in the hall and praying every night, but tonight we didn't. I think this is a test to see if we've learned anything in the five nights that we've been here."

"You may be right," Amanda replied. So, who's going to lead us in prayer.

Isabella nudges Chloe. "I think you should pray. He's listening to you, PRAY!" Before Chloe responds, Isabella pipes up and immediately nominates Chloe to pray.

"Okay, you pray, Chloe, and I will sing a song that I heard Ms. Timmons singing today."

"Lord, I'm nervous to come to you because it's been a long time. I hope you can still hear me. I just want to ask you to please be with us the rest of the night and help us do well on our presentations tomorrow."

Interrupting, "don't forget to thank him for today," whispered Isabella.

"And, yes God, thank you for allowing us to have a good day. And thank you for forgiving us of the bad things we have done. God, there is something about Ms. Timmons and this place. I've never been in a house like this before. I've never met a woman like her before. There's just something about her. It's only been five days, but it seems like we've been here five months. But, anyway, thank you and good night. Amen!"

"Amen," the girls replied in unison. Lyric begins to sing.

♪ *This little light of mine*
I'm going to let it shine
Oh, this little light of mine
I'm going to let it shine

Yolanda T. McCray

This little light of mine
I'm going to let it shine
Let it shine, let it shine! ♪

The girls depart from the circle, back to their rooms, as Lyric continues to sing. At the bottom of the stairwell stood Ms. Timmons, listening and praying the whole time.

SATURDAY MORNING— PRESENTATION DAY

Room #4

*R*ing, ring, ring... the alarm clock in Courtney's room goes off.

"Amanda, it's time to get up."

"What time is it, Courtney?"

"It's 6:30 am."

"Why are you up so early? Breakfast isn't until 9 am."

"Yes, I know, but I thought we should get up early to do any last-minute edits to our presentation."

"I finished my presentation! I'm going back to sleep. Wake me up at 7:45 am."

"Okay," Courtney said as she walked out of the room.

Bathroom Peace

Courtney walks into the bathroom and finds a note attached to the vanity mirror. "Hmmm...I wonder what this is as she opens the letter."

"Peace I leave with you, my peace I give unto you: not as the world giveth, give I unto you. Let not your heart be troubled, neither let it be afraid." John 14:27.

"Will I ever find this peace?" she said to herself as she gazed deeply into the mirror at her makeup barren, deformed face.

....

Courtney's Story...

Courtney, a once beautiful girl, was burned in a house fire caused by her drunken mother, who fell asleep while cooking at the age of 10. She suffered 3rd-degree burns on one side of her face and underwent countless corrective surgeries. Her mother died in the fire. Her neighbor rescued Courtney. Upon her mother's death, Courtney moved in with her aunt, who lived in another city. Adjusting to a new school, a new way of life, and her mother's death was overwhelming and a struggle for Courtney. This emotional roller coaster caused a spur in her relationship with her aunt. After some time, Courtney moved in with her grandmother, who lived in her hometown.

. . . .

Hometown...a place of destruction, hurt, pain, and anger! Her grandmother tried her best to get help for Courtney. She loved her very much, but Courtney built a wall around her heart so thick and placed blinders on her eyes that she could not feel or see. All she saw was ugly. All she felt was resentment. Her mirror was no longer a looking glass, but now a painful reminder of that dreaded night! Kids at school made fun of her deformed face. Courtney harvested resentment and hate in her heart toward the woman that caused her pain. A woman she once called mommy. A woman that was dead! Day in and day out, her mind was consumed with all the ugly of the world. The more she sank into this dark world, the more destructive she became to herself and others. One day while on YouTube, she discovered a makeup technique that would hide her deformities. She became obsessed with the method and the new world she found in the BIG COVER-UP! Not dealing with her true self. Not healing from old wounds. She found herself living the life of others, in any way possible or impossible.

. . . .

Girl, Recycled!

Room #3 (The door room is cracked open)

"I just heard someone walk out of the bathroom," said Chloe.

"It's about time! You better hurry up," exclaims Chloe as Isabella ran out of the room with her shower caddy.

Back in the room (Room #4)

"Girl, what took you so long in the bathroom?" Amanda said as Courtney walked back into the room.

"How do you know how long I was in there?"

"Didn't you wake me up at 6:30 am? And the time now is 7:40 am."

"Just get out the bed!" Courtney laughed trying to divert attention from herself.

"You are always up so early!"

"And look, you are still in bed, Amanda. Get up and stop talking to me girl. It's getting late."

"To be honest, I'm a little nervous, Courtney."

"Trust me, you'll be alright! Go get dress!"

Room #2

"It sounds like everyone is up. What time is it?"

"It's about 7:45 am."

"Peyton, may I ask you a question."

"It seems like you already did, Lyric."

"I'm serious."

"Okay, I'm sorry, what's up?"

"Do you think our presentations are going to go well?"

"I can only hope so."

"This project is such a strange assignment. I just wish I knew where all this is coming from."

"Listen, stop worrying. You are making me nervous."

"You're right, Peyton, but I just can't help but wonder."

"Lyric, do what you do best...SING A SONG! You will feel better."

"A song...I got it! Thank you, Peyton!"

"Huh, you got what?"

Lyric dashes out of the room.

Room #1

"Good morning, Tabitha!" announced Paige.

"Hi."

(Taking a deep breath and shaking her head, saying to herself...remember what Ms. Timmons taught you.) "Are you ready for today?"

"Are you ready?" asked Tabitha.

"I think I am. I'm a little nervous, but I think I will be alright. Thanks for asking."

At the breakfast table

The time is now 9 am, and the girls are all sitting around the table.

"Well, good morning, my princesses."

"Ms. Timmons, you called me a princess?" Peyton said in astonishment.

"Yes, baby, that's because you are. Now, who will say the Grace?"

"Ms. Timmons, may I say it," asked Tabitha. Everyone looked at each other in amazement.

"Sure, dear."

Tabitha begins to pray. "Dear Ms. Timmons's God, thank you for allowing me to be here and thank you for our food. I'm finished, Ms. Timmons."

"Well done, Tabitha! Just one thing. He's not just my God. He's your God, too, if you will let him."

"Yes ma'am."

"Now, Let's eat." The girls were frozen stiff, glaring at Tabitha as though they had seen a ghost. "Girls!" shouted Ms. Timmons. It's time to eat.

"Uh, yes, ma'am." "Sorry, Ms. Timmons," Amanda said. "We just can't believe..."

Winking her eye, Ms. Timmons politely stops Amanda from continuing her statement. "The food is getting is cold. Let's eat."

"Ms. Timmons, I am so nervous, I can't eat," said Paige.

"I am too," replied Lyric.

Suddenly, the sound of forks hitting the plates filled the room. The girls each began moaning and groaning about how nervous they were.

"Now, wait a minute, girls! What is the meaning of this? What are you so nervous?"

"We've never had to do anything like this before," Amanda sighed.

"I understand, but I'm confident you will each do a marvelous job. Just wait and see."

"If you say so, Ms. Timmons," shrugged Lyric.

"I do, now eat!"

The girls each picked up their forks reluctantly and began to eat as Ms. Timmons tried to soothe their minds.

"Okay, girls, I am going to do your morning chores for you." The room filled with joy as the girls celebrated. "I want you to take this time to prepare yourselves for the presentations." The room quickly became silent. "Lunch will be served in the Sunroom at 11:45 am this morning. Presentations will begin at 12:30 pm. So, bring all your things with you. I will see you soon."

The girls departed and went their way to prepare.

BACK TO THE GRADUATION DINNER (PRESENT-DAY)

"*I* never knew two hours could feel like two minutes," laughed Courtney.

"What are you talking about, girl?" asks Amanda.

"The morning of the presentations, remember?"

"Oh yes, you are right," chimed in Isabella. "It seemed like we had just left from breakfast and were back downstairs. That day! That was the start of healing for all of us, right, Ms. Timmons?"

"Yes, and I am so proud of you. Look what God has done for you."

"And to think, that morning when I prayed, I never knew that Ms. Timmons's God would become our God and Father too," Tabitha said smiling.

"Who was it that went first? Peyton chuckled.

"Don't be funny, Peyton!" "You knew it was me," Lyric said giving Peyton the evil eye in fun.

"I know it was you. Our little songbird was the first to take center stage."

"Yes, I was," replied Lyric—*"From Rags to a Garment of Fine Linen!"*

BACK TO THE RECYCLING PRESENTATIONS

In the Sunroom

"Come on in girls and have a seat," Ms. Timmons said with great excitement. The girls, in great amazement, basked in the beauty of the room.

"Ms. Timmons, this room is gorgeous," said Courtney.

"Thank you! I wanted to make it as beautiful and as comfortable as possible because we will be here for a while. Girls take a seat. I have snacks and drinks, and there is a restroom to your left when you need it. Let's get started... I hope that you girls learned a lot from your projects." Murmurings echoed across the room. "I know you may not understand now, but you will know before the day is over.

I've already decided the order that you will go in. When I call your name, you will stand here and present your work."

"Center stage, Ms. Timmons? Aww, man, this is going to be difficult," said Peyton.

"But you girls will do just fine. I am confident in my God. You will have time to present your work thoroughly, and afterward, we will discuss it. While one of you is presenting, the others should listen intently, making connections to your topic and life. I've also provided each of you with personalized notebooks to take notes on the different presentations. Are there any questions?"

"No ma'am," the girls responded.

"Now, let's pray."

"Dear Father, I thank you for what you are going to do through your eight princesses today. You have entrusted them to me, and I pray that you will give me the wisdom and patience to help them BE who you have called them to BE. God, please give them the strength to speak with clarity and boldness as they make their presentations. Give them listening ears and an understanding heart. Give them compassion to help each other reach their breakthroughs. I love you, Father, and I want you to be pleased with me. Please cleanse me and forgive me of the many wrongs I have done, and please let me live my life always to glorify you. In Jesus Name, Amen."

"Okay, girls. Our first presenter is Lyric."

"O please, no, Ms. Timmons."

"O, please yes, Lyric," Ms. Timmons replied as she smiled and gave a wink of confidence to Lyric. "Lyric, since you are first, you will read all the questions aloud. After that, the rest of you can choose to read or not read your questions."

"Yes, ma'am," Lyric said as she took her place on the center stage.

....

Taking a deep breath, "You all know my name is Lyric, and today I would like to introduce you to the *Clothing Station*. This morning, before breakfast, I was nervous about my project. But then, Peyton said something to me that made all the difference in the world for me. She said, Lyric, do what you do best, 'Sing a song!' So today, I am going to sing and talk."

FROM RAGS TO A GARMENT OF FINE LINEN!

First Question—Name something that is made from your product and describe its use.

I would like to introduce you to three different types of clothing by way of song and show...

♪*This is the way we dress our body, dress our body, dress our body. This is the way we dress our bodies when* ***WE LACK ATTENTION...***♪

These lyrics describe our first set of clothes that I call **THE REVEALER.**

These garments degrade who you are; they depreciate your value; they entice or draw attention in the wrong way, and they distort the true beauty of who you are inside. These are the garments of those that are searching for something. They are trying to fill a void that can't be filled through the things of this world. Hope is stolen from them. **THE REVEALER** is a cry for help. They wear these clothes because they really want to be rescued. They can pick up on a person's authenticity because they know the characteristics of users. They may fight you at first, but it's to see if you will stay around.

♪*This is the way we dress our body, dress our body, dress our body. This is the way we dress our body when **WE DON'T KNOW WHO WE ARE*** ♪

And these garments are for those that don't know if they should lean to the left or lean to the right. So that's why they are called **EDGY.**

These are the garments of the unsure. They want to fit in, but they know that the Revealer lifestyle is not for them. These are the girls that leave home one way and show up to their destination another way. These girls surrender to peer pressure while saying that they don't care what people say about me. Their disguises blind them while the inner person fights daily to resurrect. These girls are the most dangerous. They fight themselves, and they defy anyone who tries to help or bring light to their darkness.

♪ *This is the way we dress our body, dress our body, dress our body. This is the way we dress our body when* **WE KNOW WHO WE ARE** ♪

These are the garments of **THE CONCEALER.**

The person who wears these garments knows their true worth. Their beauty radiates from within to the outside, and they are the talk of the crowd. Unfortunately, many believe that her wardrobe is worth thousands, thus causing them to shy away because they feel out of her league or less valued, so they revert to the *Revealer,* unknowing that her inner beauty overshadows her clothing. These girls must be careful because one broken thread causes a hole. A hole allows unwanted things to come in. So, they must **STAY** alert. They can't afford to let their guard down. They must have someone stronger than them that encourages and keeps them daily! And, more importantly, they must know how to motivate themselves.

Clothes are sometimes the first indication of an inward problem. Teens say it's a way of expressing who they are. But as I learned through this project, it's our cry for **HELP**, in most cases.

Girl, Recycled!

....

Lyric stops to catch her breath and sips a drink of water. She noticed the girls are busy writing in their notebooks. She wonders to herself, what in the world could they be writing? She begins talking again.

....

Second Question—What does decompose mean?

Decompose has many meanings, but I chose the one that fit decomposition in clothing. For clothing, it means to separate or resolve into smaller parts or elements.

Ms. Timmons, did I do that right? So, you are doing just fine, smiled Ms. Timmons.

Okay, now for the third Question—What factors impact the decomposition process. Explain their function/purpose.

I'm sure you all found this out while doing your projects, but it blew my mind when I found out that trash has a quality rating system. The rate of decomposition depends on the structural and chemical properties of the garbage. In simpler words, it depends on how damaged or messed up something is. The other factor is temperature.

Temperature regulates the growth and activity of micro-organisms. And the third is oxygen. The oxygen present in the pores of the soil helps in the development of microorganisms. This description sounds gross, but these microorganisms eat the trash.

Fourth Question—How long does it take for your product to decompose in the environment?

If I throw my 100% cotton shirt out in the yard, it will take it six months to break down because it came from nature—a plant. For any other garments, the time is longer—20 to 200 years!

Pausing a moment and looking at her audience, Lyric begins with question five.

Describe the recycling process of your product.

First, the person must decide that they don't want their clothes anymore. Then, they either find someone to give them to or take them to places like consignment shops to be sold at bargain prices. If those two options don't work, a person can take them to a clothing recycling bin. Once collected, clothing is classified manually into three groups: reuse, rags, and fiber. The reuse clothing is baled and exported to developing countries. The rags and clothes that can be broken down to their fiber content go to the following process for further examination. Colors and material type separate them to eliminate the need for re-dying. The clothing is then torn into sloppy fibers and combined with other chosen fibers, conditioned on the planned end-use of the recycled fabric. Once cleaned and formed into thread by stretching out, twisting, and winding onto a roll, the once whole garment, now yarn is made into different things.

This goes into Question 6: Name something made after your product has been recycled and describe its use.

The recycled fibers are used in making mattresses. In addition, recyclers can send other shredded clothing to a flocking industry to produce filling material for furniture padding, panel linings, loudspeaker cones, and car insulation. So, it is possible that we are sleeping or sitting on someone's recycled clothes; or even listening to music through someone's recycled garments.

And, finally, the last question, Find the scripture in the bible that goes with the recycling process of your item.

I haven't been to church in so long, stopping her song. I felt so ashamed when I was searching for my scripture. I started thinking about how it used to be when I was much younger and how my Grandma kept us kids in church. I sang on the Sunbeam Choir. The Church is where my first love of singing began. I sing now because it takes me back to a period in my life when everything was simple. A time where my family loved each other. A time where they loved me. She said as tears rolled down her face. I used to sing then because I was thrilled. Now I sing to cover up what I'm truly feeling inside. Looking at Ms. Timmons, I'm sorry, I know that's not the question, but just like clothing, this project is breaking me down to the original contents of my life.

"Sweetheart, please continue. You are doing just fine. Don't worry about the reactions! Ms. Timmons said reassuring her.

Yes ma'am. I also thought about the kind of clothing that I wore. I started out as a concealer, but I got a hole in my garment, and because there was no guard, it kept ripping. I lost my focus because I was too busy looking at bad things. Before I knew it, I became a revealer and allowed the wrong people to see me. But it wasn't until today, through this project, that I realized that God revealed me to Ms. Timmons, so she could help me see Him. I even thought about my clothes, do I want someone else to wear my hurt clothes—for them to experience what I did—or would I want them to wear my garments of joy—the beauty within. Ms. Timmons, I've messed up for so long. I want to change my clothes. My scripture is Revelation 19:8...

And to her was granted that she should be arrayed in fine linen, clean and white: for the fine linen is the righteousness of the saints.

Will you teach me how to dress like this, Ms. Timmons? Will you teach us? The other girls shook their heads in agreement. Teach us how to care for our garments.

Thank you, guys, for listening to me.

Ms. Timmons walks over to Lyric and embraces her. The other girls all joined in as they commended her for a job well done.

"You all have a ten-minute break to use the restrooms and reset," Ms. Timmons said as the girls were talking.

BACK TO THE GRADUATION DINNER (PRESENT-DAY)

"*T*hat presentation seemed like forever, but it was only 45 minutes. It was the best 45 minutes of my life. It was the beginning of my new life. A life that counts and garments that have no holes," said Lyric.

"You are right," Courtney agreed. "You opened the door for me as I was next to take center stage…Pushing Beyond the Mask".

BACK TO THE RECYCLING PRESENTATIONS

Back in the Sunroom

"*O*kay, girls, break time is over. Next up, we will have Courtney," Ms. Timmons as she welcomed the girls back to the presentations.

Courtney takes center stage.

PUSH BEYOND THE MASK!

$\mathcal{F}$irst, I want to begin by thanking Lyric. Listening to you helped me.

Courtney takes a deep breath as she faced her audience. My product is Plastic. Masks are made from Plastic. They are used to cover up something real. Masks stop the real thing from appearing. People use them to conceal their identity because they are not happy with who they are, and by putting on a mask, the individual becomes who they want to be at any time. They use it as a disguise, not realizing that they still must deal with the natural person once the mask is off. You hide from others, but you can't hide from yourself or the ONE who created you. **MASK** is another word for **LIE**! Lies hurt, deceive, and cause mistrust, broken relationships, and a broken, distorted, confused **HEART**. Masks suffocate and seek to destroy the **TRUTH**!

Girl, Recycled!

As decomposition relates to Plastic, it means to disintegrate, which means to destroy unity or the integrity of something. It does what a mask attempts to do through the following tools: light, heat, moisture, chemical, and biological activity. The amount of light and heat will either speed up or slow down the decomposition process depending on where you are. In hotter climates, the rate is faster. In cooler temperatures, the pace is slower. Without water, the microorganisms that Lyric talked about can't grow, the soil can't be too wet or too dry. These microorganisms help the object break down into its most basic, most minor parts—thus the chemical/biological activity.

Here's the sad part, it takes 450 years for plastic masks to decompose in the open environment. Four hundred fifty years...we won't be here in 450 years. Just think about the mess that we will leave behind. The **LIES**! Turning her back to the girls, Courtney looks away, trying to conceal her tears.

"Courtney," Ms. Timmons gently calls her.

"Yes ma'am?" She replied.

"Are you okay?"

Turning to her audience and to Ms. Timmons, Courtney replies, "Yes, ma'am!" And begins where she left off.

Mounds and mounds of plastic are thrown away every year. Three hundred million tons, to be exact. Only 20% of plastics are recycled, and the other 80% makes it to the landfills to rot in the earth. What if this statistic were valid for the eight of us? That means only one of us would make it, and seven of us wouldn't—we would be left to die. Although I just met you, I don't want any of us to die. I want us to make it. Like Lyric, the recycling process begins with a collection site, then it goes to sorting, washing, shredding, and reprocessing by melting and pelletizing. This process involves the addition of fire. Plastic must first melt beyond recognition to be made into something new. Plastic in its liquid form can be broken down to paraffin wax which is found in makeup.

Suddenly, Courtney felt her face tighten and her rapidly beating. Knowing the secret she was hiding; it felt like everything was closing in on her. Finally, she grabbed her face and blurted, Ms. Timmons, may I step out for a minute before I do my scripture.

"Yes—Yes, girls, let's take a 5-minute break."

Before Ms. Timmons could get to her, Courtney runs upstairs to Bathroom Peace and stares at herself in the mirror. She reaches for the washcloth, turns the water on, and begins to wash the makeup from her face. I want the peace that you talked about, God. I'm tired of suffocating beneath this mask of makeup. Looking again into the mirror, her true self is revealed—scars and all. She put cream on her face and Vaseline on her lips and walked back downstairs to the Sunroom. She waited around the corner until the girls got inside the Sunroom. Once inside, she walked to the door, took a deep breath, and went inside. The others were talking one to another and did not notice her at first, including Ms. Timmons.

Girl, Recycled!

"Okay, girls, let's settle down," Ms. Timmons said trying to bring order to the room. She lifts her eyes and saw Courtney's face. By this time, the other girls sat in disbelief as they gazed at Courtney.

"Your—your face," Amanda said.

Interrupting, "Yes, isn't she beautiful girls?" Ms. Timmons noted with great joy.

"Me, Ms. Timmons?" Courtney said as she pointed to herself.

"Yes, you, Princess Courtney. You are beautiful," Ms. Timmons said as walked to take her seat. This compliment gave Courtney the boost she needed to continue her presentation.

I know you all are shocked to see me this way. But to be perfectly honest, I am too. I know you must have many questions, but please allow me to go into my scripture for recycling. My scripture is coming from Ezekiel 16:6-9:

And when I passed by thee, and saw thee polluted in thine own blood, I said unto thee when thou wast in thy blood, Live; yea, I said unto thee when thou wast in thy blood, Live. I have caused thee to multiply as the bud of the field, and thou hast increased and waxen great, and thou art come to excellent ornaments: thy breasts are fashioned, and thine hair is grown, whereas thou wast naked and bare. Now when I passed by thee, and looked upon thee, behold, thy time was the time of love; and I spread my skirt over thee, and covered thy nakedness: yea, I sware unto thee, and entered into a covenant with thee, saith the

Lord God, and thou becamest mine. Then washed I thee with water; yea, I thoroughly washed away thy blood from thee, and I anointed thee with oil.

The blood was my makeup. It represented my hurt and pain. The water represented renewal, cleansing, and peace. I no longer have to hide. But, the more I covered up, the deeper in a mess I got. So, when I went to the restroom and ran the water over my washcloth and then began to wipe my face, my mask started to crumble in my hand, and for the first time since the fire, I saw myself. The true ME!

The room was filled with the sounds of crying and whimpering.

Amanda leaped up and went running to Courtney, begging her forgiveness for being so mean and judgmental in the beginning.

"I forgive you, Amanda, but the truth is I caused it on myself by not being authentic to you or anyone else."

"Courtney, may I say something?" asked Paige.

"Of course."

"You look so much better now than you did before. I don't know what happened to you, but the person I'm looking at now is going to LIVE!"

"Girls, I am so proud of all of you."

"This has been a great 2 ½ hours. So, we will break here and eat a snack and chat for a while. And maybe Courtney will tell us the rest of her story," Ms. Timmons announced.

BACK TO THE GRADUATION DINNER (PRESENT-DAY)

"*W*hen we saw you without makeup, all I can remember was our mouth dropping open, Amanda said. "None of us had any idea what you were covering up. None of us knew your story until that day."

"I wonder why we always try to cover things up instead of dealing with the Truth," Tabitha said. "We are always running from the mirror. Hmmm, The Mirror..."

BACK TO THE RECYCLING PRESENTATIONS

Back in the Sunroom

B reak time is over, and the girls are ready for the next presentation.

"Next, we will have Tabitha, Ms. Timmons said as she once again corralled the girls together...

THE MIRROR: WHAT TRUTH ARE YOU LOOKING FOR?

*H*ow many of you ever heard of the old saying that you will have seven years of bad luck if you break a mirror? The girls looked around at each other and raised their hands. Well, what if you had bad luck before the mirror was broken? My station is Glass, and a mirror is made from glass. A mirror is used to reveal things or make items appear more significant than they are. Because **mirrors** reflect light, they create an illusion of open space by doubling whatever is in a room. Just like mirrors, our mind creates illusions and magnifies the bad things in our lives. One day, I became so angry with my life and all that I was going through that I took my fist and smashed the mirror in my room. Glass shattered, and blood splattered everywhere. But did anyone come to my rescue? No! Because no one was there. No one was ever there! Crying because I hurt myself, I began picking up the sharp pieces of broken glass that now covered the floor as a rug. I had to be careful where I walked because the pieces of glass were cutting my tender little feet. The sharp pieces of glass reminded me of porcupines. Porcupines have sharp pointy spines, or quills, to protect against predators. I had to find a way to defend myself, so metaphorically, I grew sharp-pointed spines to protect me against my predators—people that hurt me, fake people, people in general. My attitude became my pointy spines.

The girls looked on, listening intently. As it relates to glass, decomposition means to separate or resolve into smaller parts or elements. Like the previous two presentations, the decomposition process has three major factors that can speed up or slow down the process: the structure/makeup of the product, temperature, and the presence of oxygen. The more stuff that is put into an item, the harder it is to decompose. It takes glass one million years to decompose in an open environment. A million years! A million years of sharp attitudes!

Tabitha's head sinks into her shoulders as she hastened to the recycling process. The recycling process is as follows:

- First, glass has to be taken to a recycling center. This is the main point of collection.
- Then, it is sorted by color and washed to remove any impurities. You cannot cross-contaminate the colors. Green bottles with green bottles. Clear white bottles with clear white bottles. Brown bottles with brown bottles.
- The glass is then crushed and melted, then molded into new products such as bottles and jars. Or it may be used for alternative purposes such as brick manufacturing, fillers for paint, or decorative uses.
- The glass is then sent back to the shops, ready to be used again.

I didn't tell you this before, but glass is 100% recyclable and can be recycled endlessly without losing quality, strength, and purity. So, you must be careful with a person who is glass. Although you may clean it and change its use, the old things still live inside of it, and any little thing can trigger it to go back to its original form, to cut you again. That's why we must realize that we can't change people, and they can't change us. It's only temporal. That's why we get worn out, and if not careful, we become consumed and broken because we are trying to fix something that we can't. So, would a glass product ever change? The only way it changes is by sending it back to the Creator. He is the only one that knows what's truly inside of it. He is the only one that can change its physical and spiritual DNA; which leads me into my scripture in Jeremiah 18:1-6:

The word which came to Jeremiah from the Lord, saying, Arise, and go down to the potter's house, and there I will cause thee to hear my words. Then I went down to the potter's house, and, behold, he wrought a work on the wheels. And the vessel that he made of clay was marred in the hand of the potter: so he made it again another vessel, as seemed good to the potter to make it. Then the word of the Lord came to me, saying, O house of Israel, cannot I do with you as this potter? saith the Lord. Behold, as the clay is in the potter's hand, so are ye in mine hand, O house of Israel.

When we allow this same God to change us, we can become like paint fillers—a particular type of pigment that serves to thicken the film, support its structure and increase the volume of the paint—we will know how to support the work that God is doing in a person's life through prayer. Luke 22:32 says, when you are delivered, go deliver your sisters, and I am paraphrasing.

To end my presentation, I would like to ask each of you to forgive me, especially Paige, for how I've treated you from day one until now. God is crushing the sharp, spiny quills that I have grown, and he is making me new. I have a long way to go, but I will overcome. That's my prayer for all of you as well.

The room is filled with a roar of clapping and cheers as if they are at a game and their team has scored. Ms. Timmons shrinks back and looks to God, praising him for what he has done so far this day. It doesn't take God long to deliver when we surrender!

Walking towards the front, Ms. Timmons takes center stage, trying to gain the girls' attention. "Calm down. I know you are excited, and I am too. But we still have five more presentations to go. Lyric, Courtney, Tabitha, how do you all feel?"

In one voice, the girls shouted, "**WE FEEL GREAT**!"

"I never knew that I could feel so free, so at peace," exclaimed Courtney.

"Ms. Timmons, Ms. Timmons," interrupted Peyton. "I want to go next! Please let me go."

With a huge smile, Ms. Timmons responded, "Well, come on up! Girls let's give Peyton your full attention."

COME AND SEE!

*B*efore taking center stage, Peyton runs over to hug Tabitha, and the two of them burst into tears. "The mirror has always been my problem," Peyton proceeded to say through her tears.

"I never felt like I was good enough or pretty enough. Can anything good come out of me?" I always wondered. Walking back to center stage, she continues with her presentation. I would like to start with my scripture first, John 1:46:

And Nathanael said unto him, Can there any good thing come out of Nazareth? Philip saith unto him, Come and see.

Recycling means taking something that is of no use to someone else and makes it new. So, I invite you to come and see what Jesus has done to me and you, through this process. We thought nothing good could from us, but Jesus proved us wrong. So, come and see!

My station is Aluminum, and my product is aluminum foil. Aluminum foil is used to keep food fresh for a certain period by wrapping. Unfortunately, it takes Aluminum 80-100 years to disintegrate back into the environment. Isn't it ironic, though, Aluminum is naturally found beneath the earth's crust? It was put here by God. But mankind put extra stuff in it, causing it to take longer to break down. I believe Aluminum teaches us how to be, rather than become someone or something else. Just like Aluminum was placed naturally in the earth by God, I believe he put something inside us, a part of him, but we have messed up and allowed others to influence who we are negatively. Therefore, the recycling process is crucial for us to release the Princess that lives inside of us.

The recycling process for Aluminum begins with collecting, then sorting, and cleaning. Heat is then applied to turn the Aluminum into liquid. Finally, melting the Aluminum removes the impure coatings and chemical links added to create the aluminum product. This stage is critical because any contaminations left in the Aluminum will make it hard for it to transform into something else.

Now, let's think about this process on the human side of things. We must first become broken to allow the additives in our lives to be removed from us. Broken here means humbleness. Humbleness means to not be proud or arrogant but to be modest. So, we've got to lose the attitudes and the mask of "being hard." It doesn't work. We must meet! And, in our melting process, only skilled people should be in your inner circle during this time. People who have been transformed by God act as those fillers that Tabitha talked about. They are the ones that are praying for you and encouraging you through the word of God. They are the ones that make you mad because they tell you the truth, not what you want to hear, she says, chuckling. You don't want people that are going to slip unwelcomed influences in you.

Once the Aluminum melts, it pours into shapers that form the Aluminum into large blocks called ingots. The ingot is then sent to industrial mills where it is rolled out to gain greater flexibility and strength. Each bar can be used to make about 1.6 million drink cans.

Let's pause there for a moment. Whew, that's a lot of processing! I wonder what would've happened if we all ran to Jesus first instead of other things? God can re-make us to be larger and more robust than we ever were before if we **HUMBLE** ourselves!

I never knew how this project would change my life, my outlook on things. I mean, God and I have a lot of work to do, but we've all made that first step, although unwillingly, we are at the collection site. I know that I am a **Princess** now, his **Princess**. She just needs to be released inside of me! That's me. I'm done, well, I mean, I'm just beginning.

But I'm done with my presentation, she said with a vibrant smile as she took her seat.

"This presentation deserves a song," chimes Lyric. "Not a coverup song, but a really true melody. May I sing, Ms. Timmons?"

Ms. Timmons nods her head with a smile and a thumbs up.

The girls stand up as Lyric began to sing...

♪*We are free*
Praise the Lord; we're free
No longer bound,
No more chains holding us,
Our soul is resting,
Praise the Lord,
Hallelujah, we're FREE!!!!! ♪

"Sing it one more time Lyric," shouted Peyton as the other girls joined in...

♪*We are free*
Praise the Lord; we're free
No longer bound,
No more chains holding us,
Our soul is resting,
Praise the Lord,
Hallelujah, we're FREE!!!!! ♪

"When you are ready, you are ready! Great job, Peyton! Before I make my next selection, does anyone want to volunteer," Ms. Timmons said as she looked over the room.

Amanda raises her hand. "I would like to go next."

"Come on up and take center stage. Your audience awaits your presentation," Ms. Timmons responded.

BROKEN CRAYONS
STILL COLOR!

"*M*s. Timmons, I really thought this project was ridiculous, and I felt that you were a strange lady. I ask that you please forgive me because now I know better."

"You are forgiven Amanda," Ms. Timmons said in a gentle and reassuring voice.

"Thank you so much," Amanda replied. "My eyes are open, and I am beginning to see things a whole lot clearer. What I thought was true wasn't true at all! The very people that were fighting for me, I was fighting against."

Well, hey y'all, Amanda said as she turned towards her audience. My station is Crayons. Did you know that broken crayons still color? When I was younger, I was fascinated with crayons. The colors were so pretty and vibrant, and they made my drawings come to life. I protected my crayons and was very careful not to break them. Because, after all, everyone knew once a crayon was broken, it was of no use. It just didn't color the same. That was my mindset. Therefore, I went through many boxes of crayons in my life, sorting through the many boxes to find the broken ones, so I could replace them or ask for a new box of crayons. I wanted my crayons to be perfect—sharp, not dull, and easy to color with. Once they got a certain length, I would not use the crayons anymore. Man, I would sit for hours drawing and coloring. I started with coloring books, then graduated to creating my own pictures. My parents were very supportive and encouraged me to keep drawing. My mom framed my drawings and hung them on the walls of my room. Life for me was GREAT! I had parents who loved me and siblings who were my best friends. They were each like a crayon in my box. I protected them and was very careful not to break, hurt or use them up because I wanted them always to be full of color.

Paige, interrupting Amanda, "So what happened? Why are you here with us?"

"My crayon broke," Amanda replied, "And I didn't know how to put it together again."

The girls looked at each other and shrugged their shoulders in confusion.

"So, you are here because your crayon broke?" Paige said in disbelief.

"Settle down and let her finish girls," Ms. Timmons interjected.

Regrouping herself, Amanda continued. I know this all sounds crazy right now, but I will get to my point. Like I was saying, my crayon was broken into pieces. And, not just one, but all five of them, my family, but not my family. You see, I didn't tell you all that I am adopted, but I wasn't supposed to find out, at least not in the way that I did. My siblings and I went to stay with my grandparents one weekend. A lady came by to drop off a cake to my Grandma while we kids were outside playing in the backyard. I went into the house to ask Grandma to come and play with us, just like she always did. As I walked in, I overheard the lady say to my Grandma; I'm glad to see how Amanda fits in with the other children. I didn't understand what that meant. Why would I have to fit in? They are my sisters and brother. I hid in the corner and continued to listen to the conversation. She then said, some of us in the neighborhood were against Cynthia, my mom, adopting a child, especially a drug baby. But we were wrong. She's grown up to be a pretty girl. What did your Grandma say to her? Well Clara, Grandma said, I never knew you all felt that way about my daughter and her family. Thank you for telling me. Then, Grandma handed her back the cake and told her to leave the house and never return. She was not welcome in her home anymore. When Grandma came back from seeing the lady to the door, she saw me stooped in the corner of the kitchen crying uncontrollably. At that moment, my family of crayons suddenly became broken. We've heard from the previous presentations that when an object decomposes, it breaks down into the essential ingredients that made it whole. In my mind, I didn't come from them, so, therefore, how could I be a part of them. I felt like I was the contaminated piece that got into the mixture by accident.

The Sunroom suddenly became quiet. The girls were speechless.

Adopted—not an original part—and a drug baby! I was on drugs before I knew what drugs were. My once vibrant crayon box suddenly became dull!

Proceeding with her story...Amanda, my grandmother cried out to me, baby, what's wrong? I heard what that lady said: Grandma, is my mommy and daddy really not my mommy and daddy? She tried to console me, but I was overcome with grief and did the only thing I knew to do at the time, run away. I remember her calling out to my sisters, telling them to go after me. They were confused, but they chased me down and brought me back to the house. By that time, my aunts and uncles were at my Grandma's house. Later that night, my mom and dad left their trip and came to get us. I remember crying, and all I would say to anyone was that lady broke my crayons.

From that day, my life spun out of control. I was always so careful not to break my crayons because a broken crayon was of no use. I constantly tossed them aside. The color was no longer vibrant. And they were hard to manage. Unlike the hundreds of years it takes a crayon to break down in the open environment, it only took my life thirteen years. Yes, I was thirteen years old when I found out. I separated myself from my siblings and my parents. I built a wall around myself, despite my family's endless efforts to reassure me of their love for me. I stopped drawing and hadn't held a crayon in my hand until now. I hurt the only people that loved me and cared for me. So, how did I end up here? I stopped coloring. Because my birth mom gave me up and fed me drugs, I must've been broken and worthless—of no actual use or purpose. I forgot the last thirteen years of my life and convinced myself that I was no good.

I had that stuck in my mind. Tabitha, as you said, my mind was my mirror—speaking falsehoods and magnifying those lies. I went through counseling but to no avail. As each day went by, I slipped deeper and deeper in this gray, hazy place. I became harmful to myself. I started cutting to numb the pain that I felt inside. My parents tried to help me, but I would lash out at them. The very people that we're fighting for me, I fought against. My parents couldn't help me, and they became afraid that they would wake to my death one morning.

Ms. Timmons walked over to Amanda and gently held her hand. "Are you okay, Princess?"

"Yes, ma'am," she replied.

"Do you want to finish?"

"If I don't know, I'm afraid that I won't later."

Ms. Timmons smiles and walks back to her seat.

This place, I know now, is very different than any place that I have been. I think it was Lyric that said this is our collection point. All of us are broken crayons that have been collected. We are being sorted by our different colors—which are our **STORIES**. Once sorted, the broken crayons are boosted with more pigment to emphasize the tone of the original color. I believe that **HOPE** is our boost. The crayon bits are then shredded down into smaller pieces and placed in an oven under extreme heat. Once melted, it is poured into molds that shape the crayons; and once chilled, they are removed from their molds and are ready to use. For the first time, I believe that I am going to **COLOR** again!

The scripture that I chose for this process is Jeremiah 29:11 (NIV):

For I know the plans I have for you," declares the Lord, "plans to prosper you and not to harm you, plans to give you hope and a future.

I've been recycled twice. The first time was when God delivered me from my birth mom—He gave me a better future; and now, from my own self-destruction—He delivered me from my own harm. I have an activity for you; she said as she gave each girl a blank sheet of paper and allowed them to pick their favorite color from a box of new, vibrant crayons. Does everyone have a crayon? The girls all shook their heads, yes. Okay. I want you to draw a big heart in the center of your paper and color it. The girls all drew their hearts and colored just as Amanda instructed. Now, I want you to break your crayon in half on my count. Bracing herself for the once terrifying sound, Amanda placed her favorite purple crayon between her thumb and forefinger of both hands and counted to three. One...two... three...Now break your crayons. You could hear pops echoing throughout the room as the girls broke their crayons.

A once terrifying sound now became the first drum beat to the cadence of **HOPE**! This same **HOPE** is the color booster of our lives. Tears began to roll down Amanda's face. "Are you okay, Amanda?" asked Paige. Opening her eyes, Amanda responded, I am. I actually am. Please draw another heart and color. Now break the crayon again, draw a heart and color. The girls repeated breaking the crayons three times. Now, look at your picture of hearts. Are there any color differences? No, responded the girls. Can you tell which piece of crayon you used for each?

"Not really, but the smaller the crayon became, the more challenging it was to draw and color the heart," said Courtney.

"Yes, but it caused us to be more careful of what we were doing, but we got the job done," said Tabitha.

"And, for me, the last heart that we drew is the one I am most proud of because drawing the other hearts was easy," Lyric chimed in.

"I got it!", exclaimed Chloe. "Just because we are broken doesn't mean that life has to stop. It doesn't mean that we are no longer valuable. Instead, we must tear down those inappropriate images that present themselves as **TRUTH**."

"Yes, we have some work to do. So, don't stop coloring," Amanda said. With a sigh of relief, Ms. Timmons, I am finished.

"No, dear, you are just beginning. All of you are, my Princesses!!!" Ms. Timmons continues, "Ok, girls, we have three more presentations to go. It is now 4:45 pm. I have dinner being catered in for us today. It should be here at 5 pm. So, let's get freshen up and take a little break. We are going to eat on the patio tonight, so we'll meet there at 5:15 pm."

The girls left the room, but Paige stayed behind.

YOUR BROKEN PIECES FOR HIS WHOLENESS!

"*A*ll this talk about broken crayons, really? "What happens when the pieces become too small to hold, unmanageable and scattered?" Paige said to herself as she watched the other girls walk away.

"Paige, aren't you coming?" Tabitha called out to her as she stood in a daze.

"Uh, yes, I'll catch up with you guys in a few."

"In a few? What's going on, Paige?" asked Tabitha.

"Now, why are you in my business Tabitha?"

"I'm not; I just...

Interrupting Tabitha, Paige spouted off, "You just what?!" You know what, with her hands flailing in the air, I just can't do this anymore, yelled Paige!

Girl, Recycled!

"What can't you? Talk to me!" Tabitha replied.

Paige immediately ran out the Sunroom door onto the patio. Tabitha goes after her, but Paige continues to run.

Frantically, Tabitha yells for Ms. Timmons and the other girls. Hearing the commotion, they all came running outside. "Tabitha, what happened?"

"I don't know, but she's getting away. We must catch her." Looking up, they saw Paige running, and they all took off after her.

"Paige, Paige, where are you going?" shouted the others. Paige continued to run when suddenly, she tripped and fell to her knees. The girls and Ms. Timmons were finally able to catch her.

"Paige!" shouted Amanda; "why did you run?"

"What's wrong?" Peyton said as she panted for her breath.

"Oh, Ms. Timmons, they hurt me! They hurt me! Paige cried.

"I got you, Princess, Ms. Timmons said as she fell to her knees to embrace Paige. It's going to be alright now. I'm here now, and we won't let anyone hurt you.

Paige squeezed her; "Promise me you won't let them hurt me again."

"Paige," Ms. Timmons said as she brushed the hair from her eyes, "listen to me, God brought you here, so he could heal you and take away your hurt. He'll do it for you if you let him in."

"Let him in?"

"Into your heart, sweetie."

"How can he come into a heart that is shattered?" cried Paige. "I am crushed, and I don't know how to put myself back together again. I feel like the particles of my life have decomposed and are scattered everywhere, and I will never be made whole."

"Listen to me; you can't put yourself together Paige."

"I can't, Ms. Timmons? So, what's going to happen to me?" She said as she continued to sob.

"Sweetie, what I mean is that none of us can fix ourselves. We must submit to God and let him do it. He wants to do it. He's the only one that can. Oh, baby girl, he's the Master at doing the impossible. Psalms 34:18 says, *The Lord is close to the brokenhearted and saves those who are crushed in spirit. (N.I.V.)* Will you let Him into your life?"

"You mean, now?

"There's no time like the present."

Wiping her tear-soaked face, Paige responds, "I want Him to heal me. I want to be fixed. I want him in my life. I want to color."

"Repeat after me," Ms. Timmons said to Paige...

Father, I am hurt
I am broken
I am crushed
What's left of me

Please come inside of me and do the impossible.
I want you to. I need you to.
I surrender to your power.
Help me to learn of You, Your Mercy, and Your Grace.

....

If you are reading this book and want God to heal your heart, you can pray the same prayer as Paige did with humbleness and sincerity, and Jesus will come into your heart. This is the first step to your healing process. It may get hard at times but don't ever forget what you just did. Jesus wants to and can heal you completely. Healing is a process, and it takes a little time. How long it takes depends on your attitude. Bad attitudes tend to prolong the process.

H = Help (Learn to accept the help that God sends to you.)

E = Edify (Allow God to rebuild you—enjoy the process.)

A = Attitude (Attitude is everything, we must have a positive, faith-full attitude)

L = Live (Life begins with God, so now that He is in your life—LIVE! Don't just exist!)

....

"Girls, help me get her up," summoned Ms. Timmons.

"I think I twisted my ankle," moaned Paige.

"Tabitha, you and Courtney get on either side of her and walk her back to the house. The rest of you girls go wash up and meet me on the patio."

"I guess the old girl still has it—these legs of mine still can run," Ms. Timmons said to herself, laughing as she walked back to the house.

BACK TO THE GRADUATION DINNER (PRESENT-DAY)

"*B*oy, we never thought Ms. Timmons could run so fast," the girls laughed. That was a day!

I bet you will never forget that run, Paige.

"You got a bruised knee and a twisted ankle," Tabitha said laughing.

"I even have the scar to remind me," Paige said.

"So, what was your station again? Foam. Oh yea, I guess you thought you could just float away, huh? Courtney jokingly said.

"Ha, ha, ha!" Paige replied. She continues, "You know, when I look back at it, it's the fluff that gets us into trouble.

All that extra stuff. Take the foam, for instance. Remember, I told you all that only about 5% of a foam package is polystyrene. The rest is air. Because foam is so light, it's hard to collect from curbside containers—it often blows away, becoming litter. Think about the stuff made from foam like cups, plates, carry-out trays, etc. Always on the side of roads, you see a lot of this stuff because it has blown off trucks or people throw them out of car windows. When we really look at it, all of us were made of foam at one time...We had no sustenance, tossed and driven, bouncing from one person or thing to another. Once we were tossed aside, we were carried away by every wind that blew.

Pausing for a moment and looking at everyone, Paige's tone became very serious as she continued to speak. "But there was a strange wind that blew one day and gathered us all to a place that removed the fluff from our lives and gave us the Word of God! Our foundation and nurturing are in Jesus Christ. Thank you, Mama Timmons. Because you never gave up on me, I made it. But as you have taught us, all glory and honor belongs to God and I am so thankful that he loved and loves me! I now have a new heart, built more robust than ever before. My hurt has been healed, and my filth has been taken away."

BACK TO THE RECYCLING PRESENTATIONS

Back in the Sunroom

"*M*s. Timmons, that was a great dinner!" Isabella said.

"Thank you, my dear," Ms. Timmons replied. "Let's get settled. We had three presentations left, but God had a different plan for us. Healing comes in all forms and ways. So, now we are down to our finale, with two presentations left. Isabella, I would like you to go next, and Chloe, you will close us out."

GIVE US THIS DAY,
YOUR DAILY BREAD!

J don't know about you guys, but for me, this has been a compelling day, with a unique workout thanks to Paige. All the girls giggled. No, but seriously though, I am so thankful. Sometimes, we have to become broken for God to put us together the right way. Sometimes, we have to become damaged, so what is inside us can flow: without walls, borders, or barriers. That's weird to say, but the evidence is here in this room. Once we have been set free of the mess, we must be re-filled with the right kind of stuff. Mark 5:43 reads:

And he charged them straitly that no man should know it; and commanded that something should be given her to eat.

Girl, Recycled!

Something to eat... Hmmmmm... My station is Food. Food is used to nourish the human body. It is used to prevent us from starvation. Starvation means suffering or death caused by hunger. I used to be hungry. My mom fell into hard times and I, being the oldest, tried to feed my brother and sister. I would hang out at bakeries and restaurants, waiting for them to throw out their leftover food. Then, I would quickly retrieve it and take the food home to eat because I didn't want us to starve to death. This went on for a few months until I was caught by the police, who were waiting for me one day. A DSS home inspection was ordered, and we were taken away from my mom. It's been a year since I've seen my brother and sister and mom, and I miss them very much.

I knew the exact time they took things to the dumpster. I was careful to be there at that exact time because if food stays out in the open too long, it begins to rot or decay, giving off an offensive odor. This is the beginning of decomposition. A smell that attracted flies, pests, and rodents. When the flies come, they begin to lay maggots that eat away at the food, breaking it down even further. The hotter the temperature, the quicker the food decomposes. Unlike the other stations, it only takes food two weeks to two months to decay. It all depends on the contents of the food product.

Food waste makes up about 30% of the average home's garbage. Just think about all the food we waste daily. But there is a new life for leftovers. Recycling food is called composting.

What do you think the first step of recycling food is? The girls all exclaimed…"Collection!"

You're right. The food is collected. Then it goes through a machine where metals and other inorganic waste are removed. The food is then compressed, and micro-organisms or bacteria are used to speed up decomposition. To help limit odors, the compressed food goes through an aeration process—where food scrap is turned constantly to allow oxygen to flow through—a heavy plastic is used as a covering. Once the process is finished, a material called compost is created. Compost is rich in nutrients. It is used in gardens, landscaping, horticulture, and farming. The compost conditions the soil, acting as a fertilizer. That's the science of recycling food.

Now, let's go back to the scripture I began with. The little girl was dead, but Jesus brought her back to life, even though the bystanders doubted him. There are people in our lives, whether intentional or unintentional, who are not expecting us to live. They have seen us rot away and smelled the offensive odors we have given off through our bad attitudes, numbness, lack of understanding, disrespect, hurt, and the list goes on. But after today, I realized that it wasn't physical food that I needed more than anything. It was the Word of God, the food that does not rot or decay but keeps on producing and nurturing. I know I will see my family again, and when I do, I will do as Jesus instructed the little girl's parents to do. I will feed them. I will teach them a new way of eating. I will give them food that will teach them how to never go hungry again. I will provide them with what was given to me, on this day, **THE WORD OF GOD**!!!

The girls all stood clapping and cheering!!!!!

"Great job, Isabella!" Ms. Timmons walked to the center of the room. "Well, ladies, we are almost at the finish line. Chloe, you are next. Bring us to home plate."

WRITTEN TO BE READ!

𝓔 xtra, extra, read all about it! I am the Paper Station. But wait, I must first warn you, what you are about to read is troubling. Life has been taken, and I am responsible. The girls, on the edge of their seats, looked at Ms. Timmons. She notices their looks and reassures them with a smile that everything was going to be ok. Then, Chloe hands a newspaper article to Isabella. Will you please read the title of the article?

"*GIRL KILLED IN CAR CRASH*;" Isabella read aloud as she passed the paper to the other girls.

And I, Chloe, am the sole survivor. Pausing a moment as she fought back her tears she said, as well as the **KILLER**. The girls looked on, ears perched, waiting for Chloe's next words.

At the age of sixteen, a trip to the grocery store turned tragic. My parents allowed me to drive to the store, which was a short distance from my house. I was supposed to go straight there and back, but instead, I called my best friend Tonya to see if she wanted to ride with me. I picked her up, and we were off to the store. On our way back, I received a text message, and while responding, I lost control of the car. The next thing I knew, I was in a hospital. And shortly after that, I was attending the funeral of my best friend. My whole life changed in a matter of minutes.

I couldn't deal with the pain and agony that I was going through. It should have been me that died instead of her. We were so close. We did everything together. Everywhere I turned, that article haunted me. I didn't want to go back to school because I felt like everyone was mad at me for killing Tonya. I didn't want to go out in public for fear that people would recognize me. I was marked for life. I let my parents down. I took Mr. and Mrs. Daniels' only daughter away from them forever. I let myself down. I let God down. I was grieving and mourning for my friend and myself. I went into a deep depression and lost my will to live. I stopped talking. I was placed in and out of observation homes because I required 24-hour observation and care. The doctors told my parents that soon, I would be admitted to a permanent mental institution if I didn't make any progress. But my mom and dad fought for me on their knees through prayer. One day the nurse came into my room, and she told me that I was being moved. They packed me up, and I ended up here.

One day I wish to see that newspaper article disintegrate into small pieces as the definition of decomposition suggests, but I know that will come in time. Ms. Timmons, that prayer closet, I wanted to go inside so badly, but I was afraid. Then one night, it felt like that room was calling me, and I went. There I spent most of the night crying and pouring out to God. He reminded me of what was written in my heart. His WORD! The Lord saved Tonya and me when we were younger. The Church was our life, and I lost my way. But I had to come here to find my way again. He took me to Jeremiah 31:32-33:

Behold, the days come, saith the Lord, that I will make a new covenant with the house of Israel, and with the house of Judah: Not according to the covenant that I made with their fathers in the day that I took them by the hand to bring them out of the land of Egypt; which my covenant they brake, although I was an husband unto them, saith the Lord: But this shall be the covenant that I will make with the house of Israel; After those days, saith the Lord, I will put my law in their inward parts, and write it in their hearts; and will be their God, and they shall be my people.

This certainly was me. I broke my covenant with God. Instead of running to him, I ran away from him. But I'm so glad that he chose to recycle my newspaper, take my heart piece by piece, and write his word on it as he heals me. I hope he does this for all of us! Thank you! The girls run to embrace her.

Girl, Recycled!

"Can we all get in a circle?" Ms. Timmons said as she walked to the front of the room? "Let's pray."

Father, I can't begin to thank you for all you have done for us on this day.

You have begun a great work in these girls, and I am so grateful.

You have allowed me to witness their spiritual beginnings with you. I pray that they never forget what happened today, and it would forever be written on the tablets of their hearts. In Jesus' name. Amen!

"Girls, we have had a full day, and I am so proud of you. I want you to know that I love you, and I will be here to walk with you as you begin your journeys. Don't take what has happened here lightly or for granted. You all made an essential step today towards your deliverance. And I am so glad that I got to experience those steps with you. I have provided each of you with a journal and a personalized bible. Write, read, study! Always keep them near to you, ok?"

"Yes, ma'am!" the girls said in unison.

"Ok. Let's get ready for bed. Breakfast will be at 8am tomorrow morning. Then, we all will go to Church at 10am. It's 9:00pm now, so go get some rest, and I will see you Princesses in the morning."

"Good night," the girls said as they departed.

"Good night babies and sweet dreams," Ms. Timmons said with the biggest smile on her face.

In Ms. Timmons' Room

Ms. Timmons breaks out into a shout and tears of joy as she fell to her knees, overwhelmed by all that her eyes beheld, her ears heard, and her heart felt. "Father, thank you so much for doing the work in those girls. It doesn't take you long to do what you do when we have been obedient to you. Thank you for your grace and mercy. I know those girls have a long road ahead of them, but I know they will be alright if you go before them. Help me to hold out and do and be who you need me to be to them during this process. I love you, Lord! I love you, Lord! I knew you would come through for your servant!"

BACK TO THE GRADUATION DINNER (PRESENT DAY)

"*Mama* Timmons, we heard you that night after the presentations," Tabitha said. "I came down to get something from downstairs, and I heard a noise. I thought something was wrong. So, I called for the other girls, and they all came running downstairs, and we stayed at your door that night, rejoicing and crying with you. We felt a love and a presence like we never felt in our lives."

"Really, girls, I didn't know you were there," said Ms. Timmons.

"Yes, ma'am, we were," Peyton said.

"That was the night that you became Mama Timmons to us," said Paige. "A lady who just met us actually cried for us. You will never know how your prayer changed our lives that night."

"We've all gone through so much over the past years and have grown tremendously, haven't we, Mama Timmons?" Amanda asked.

"Yes, you certainly have, and I am thrilled to see that God has healed yours and others' wounds," she said as she turned to Chloe. "I saw Mr. and Mrs. Daniels give you a hug, Chloe. That was the picture of God's grace."

"Yes, it was. They told me that they were waiting on me to forgive myself for what happened. I was the one that did wrong. I took their daughter away, and they were waiting on me. Mama Timmons, that's the part of God that I will never understand. No matter what we go through or have done in our lives, he's willing to forgive us."

"You are so right."

"That's just mind-blowing," responded Amanda. "And because He forgives, we MUST forgive others."

"When I think about the time wasted and lost for my life, just because I refused to forgive my mom and all that I went through makes me angry and at the same time makes me want to ensure that I never waste another minute, that I only trust God for the things that I cannot change," said Courtney.

"With that mindset, my dear, you will go F.A.R.— Forgive & Restore," said Mama Timmons.

"Do you guys remember what Mama Timmons told us weeks after the presentation?" Peyton asked...

ONE MONTH AFTER THE PRESENTATIONS

"*H*ey girls, summer is almost over, and I wanted to pull my Princesses together to talk. I've had one-on-one meetings with each of you, and we've discussed so much at great lengths. I've seen your growth in the almost 2-1/2 months that you've been here, and I am so proud of each of you. I gave you a month to reflect and absorb what took place during the Recycle presentations. So, today we are going to dig a little deeper as a team."

"After the questions, Mama Timmons, will you share your thoughts on our presentations and the changes we've made since then?" Peyton asked.

"Yes, I will," said Mama Timmons.

Girl, Recycled!

My first question...What recycling process step did each of your products have in common?

"Can I go first, Mama Timmons?" Lyric asked?

"Sure...and whoever wants to go next, just chime in," said Mama Timmons.

"They all go through a **SEPARATING** process."

"Yes, and they all must be **CLEANSED**," said Amanda.

"Likewise, they all use **HEAT** to **TRANSFORM** them into something else," said Peyton.

"Don't forget that they all must be **DEFACED** or **DISFIGURED**, as well," said Courtney.

"Excellent observations, girls," Mama Timmons said.

Here's my next question...What impact does this process have on your life?

"I have to become "disfigured" to be "configured," Tabitha said. "I've spent a lot of time around things that have contaminated me and caused me to become all out of whack, but God has allowed this process, so he can rebuild me, better and stronger than before."

"For me, Ms. Timmons," Paige said. "I have to be emptied out of my old self, hence the cleansing, to be filled with a new life in God."

"To be new, I had to be separated—that's why God chose me to be adopted because he had a better life waiting for me," said Amanda. "Heat is needed to melt a product down. Once the product is dissolved, it can easily be re-made. Here is the heat! Right here is where we will be treated, ready for production, ready to be made NEW."

"For me, it's a new headline that reads **FORGIVEN**!" exclaimed Chloe!

"You've all answered well, and I am so glad that you can see those things now. Let me tell you all something, God brought you here for a reason. I want to go back to Courtney's scripture in Ezekiel 16:6. Do you all remember it? Let me read it to you again:"

And when I passed by thee, and saw thee polluted in thine own blood, I said unto thee when thou wast in thy blood, Live; yea, I said unto thee when thou wast in thy blood, Live.

"When you all thought that no one saw you, when you felt that your cries were not heard, my Savior heard you. Not only did he listen to you, but he also prepared a place for you. A place that would allow him to be LORD and let him WORK! Amanda, you were right. This is the PLACE—A CONTROLLED ENVIRONMENT. Just as God heard and saw you in your mess, he was preparing me for you. You see, girls, I had to overcome many obstacles in my life. Some I caused and some I did not cause. But through every form of opposition, God was glorified. Just like you, he emptied me out of my old self and made me be the woman he needed me to be. A woman that would answer the call to help His girls, His Princesses."

"The first day that you came began day one of your healing process—the RECYCLING PROCESS. When I told you to go to your stations, I heard the murmurings. I listened to the complaints. But I couldn't let that stop me from what God instructed me to do. That was the day of sorting, but you all huddled in one corner—refusing to be sorted, refusing to stand alone. I knew you had no idea of who you were or what was going on, but He did. That's how you got your assignments. All you saw was the image of what appeared to be you, but not you. Your view of who you are was distorted through the stuff—life's mess—that was covering you. You saw everyone and everything that ever hurt you."

"You girls had *landfill syndrome*. Landfill syndrome, said the girls? So many girls end up in landfills, a deep hole dug in the earth where layers upon layers of trash are dumped. Trash becomes the earth's blanket. A place where the birds feed and pestilence live. God wants to deliver you from the landfills of your life. He wants to change your blanket of despair and hopelessness, of vain beauty and emptiness, and of anger and bitterness. He wants to cover you in his blanket of LOVE—real, everlasting LOVE! Did you know the CROSS is the ULTIMATE RECYCLING STATION for human beings—for you and me? Jesus took every bad thing that we've ever done and the ones we haven't done yet, and took them on the CROSS, cleansed our soul with his blood, and made us all new!!!!! He paid the price for us all!

Your projects are a parable. "A parable?" Tabitha asked.

"Yea, you know, a story that helps you see a spiritual truth more clearly," Amanda explained.

"That's correct. Your projects weren't about the product at all. They were designed to help you see yourself more clearly. I can see a shift in your mindset. The scales are falling off your eyes, and you can see your life clearer. You are beginning to see your potential of who you can and were meant to BE! Every day you are going to have to make a choice to continue the process. Some days are going to be complicated. Some days are going to be easy. Some days are going to be no feelings at all. But just as the products that you were assigned did not fight against its recycling process, you can't fight against yours. God will place the right people in your life to remind and challenge you to always do what is right. There's a lot that we must learn together!"

"We, Ms. Timmons?" Peyton asked.

"Yes, baby girl, WE. I am in this with you," replied Ms. Timmons. "For however long it takes—**WE WILL MAKE IT!**"

At the Graduation Dinner

"*And* WE MADE IT! ALL OF US!!!

"Yes, you girls did. I have one more gift for you," said Ms. Timmons as she handed each girl a box.

"Another gift," exclaimed Isabella?

"But you've given us so much over the years," said Lyric.

"That's what a servant does, Princesses," said Mama Timmons in a humble voice.

"I can't wait to see what's inside," Chloe said as she ripped the wrapping off the box.

"A crown," Mama Timmons?

"This is so beautiful. I got one too," shouted Tabitha!

"And us too," the others exclaimed. The girls began to show their crowns. All were different.

"Wait a minute, this fabric looks familiar," said Peyton. And isn't this a piece of my old cell phone?

The others began to see very familiar things in each of their crowns that they had experienced throughout their life. Chloe's newspaper article, a picture of Courtney's birth mother, Isabella's siblings, Lyric's old songs, a mirror for Tabitha, a broken crayon for Amanda, and a broken heart for Paige were all carefully woven into the beauty of the crown.

"We don't understand Mama Timmons. Why would you make a crown like this?"

"Let me read a scripture to you ladies."

To bestow on them a crown of beauty instead of ashes... Isaiah 61:3

I kept remnants of the things that brought you to me. Those things were designed by Satan to destroy you, but God took the ashes of your life and made you a Princess fit for a Crown. You will one day run into a girl experiencing different challenges in their life, and my prayer is that you will help guide them. You will share the story of your crown of beauty and how you made it through and help them to make a crown for themselves.

"We never knew something so ugly could be made into something so beautiful. The details and the time it must have taken you to make them mean so much to us," Isabella said. "What was meant to kill us, God turned it around for our good!!!!"

"What an AWESOME God we serve!" sung Lyric.

The girls embraced each other and continued to share in their celebration and stories of old.

....

There are many Princesses that God is waiting and wanting to heal. But they feel like God, or no one else sees them. Matthew 23:37 N.I.V. reads:

Jerusalem, Jerusalem, you who kill the prophets and stone those sent to you, how often I have longed to gather your children together, as a hen gathers her chicks under her wings, and you were not willing.

God longs for you—his desire is to have you as his own—but sometimes we fight him and refuse the help he sends.

So, I beg you today, my Princesses, STOP FIGHTING and let God FIGHT FOR YOU! I know you are probably saying that people are *fake*, and they just want to get in your business, and while sometimes that is true, that is not the case for all. The person that God sends will come thoroughly equipped to help you through your process—they will come with HIS WORD—not to belittle you, but to LIFT you, and they will invite you to follow them as they follow CHRIST—our MODEL!

Will you become a ***GIRL RECYCLED*** today? The first step is to remove yourself from your sources of contamination.

Girl, Recycled!

Where is your collection point? Even if you can't move physically, remove yourself mentally and surrender to God! Get in His Holy Word—this is the cleansing stage—His Word is our spiritual soap. Empty yourself to Him by pouring out all your pain, hurt, wrongdoings, misunderstandings, etc.—this is Confession! Once you have confessed, A.S.K. him to come and dwell in your life. BELIEVE, even if your heart is shattered—remember the crayon—that Jesus Christ died for your wrongdoings, and He lives to heal and cleanse you! Once you have done this, let Him re-create you! And don't forget, when you have been restored, be led by God to go help someone else.

AUTHOR BIO

*Y*olanda McCray, a servant of God and published author, is a native of Georgetown, South Carolina. She is a graduate of Clemson University with a Bachelor of Science in Electrical Engineering. After working as an engineer for ten years, she was led by God to resign from her position and focus on the healthy development of girls. She does this through life coaching, leadership, and self-efficacy workshops, mentoring and public speaking. In addition, Yolanda is the Girls' Ministry Leader at her church, New Light Missionary Baptist, where she serves faithfully. Her life's motto is, "I used to engineer products, now I spiritually engineer girls through God's leading."

Made in the USA
Columbia, SC
05 November 2021